Herb Wharton was born in Cunnamulla, Queensland, and began working as a drover in his teenage years. His maternal grandmother was of the Kooma people; his grandfathers were Irish and English. In 1992 with the publication of his first book, *Unbranded*, he committed to novel form his experiences of his long years spent on the stock routes of inland Australia. *Cattle Camp*, a collection of droving histories as told by Murri stockmen and women, was published in 1994. *Where Ya' Been Mate?*, a collection of short stories, followed in 1996.

Herb has travelled extensively throughout Australia and abroad. In 1998, he was selected for a residency at the Australia Council studio in Paris where he completed *Yumba Days*, his first book for young readers. He was awarded the Australia Council Award for Lifetime Achievement in Literature in 2012, and most recently was the recipient of a black&write! Fellowship in 2022.

First Nations Classics

UNBRANDED

HERB WHARTON

UQP

First published 1992 by University of Queensland Press
PO Box 6042, St Lucia, Queensland 4067 Australia
Reprinted 1994, 1996, 2000, 2010, 2012, 2018, 2019
This First Nations Classics edition published 2023

University of Queensland Press (UQP) acknowledges the Traditional Owners
and their custodianship of the lands on which UQP operates. We pay our
respects to their Ancestors and their descendants, who continue cultural and
spiritual connections to Country. We recognise their valuable contributions
to Australian and global society.

uqp.com.au
reception@uqp.com.au

Cover design by Jenna Lee
Author photograph by Farley Ward
Typeset in 11.5/16 pt Bembo Std by Post Pre-press Group, Brisbane
Printed in Australia by McPherson's Printing Group

  First Nations Classics are assisted
by the Australian Government through
the Australia Council, its arts funding
and advisory body.

This project is supported by the Copyright Agency's Cultural Fund.

CULTURAL FUND

A catalogue record for this book is available from the National Library of Australia.

ISBN 978 0 7022 6596 9 (pbk)
ISBN 978 0 7022 6783 3 (epdf)
ISBN 978 0 7022 6784 0 (epub)

University of Queensland Press uses papers that are natural, renewable and
recyclable products made from wood grown in well-managed forests and
other controlled sources. The logging and manufacturing processes conform
to the environmental regulations of the country of origin.

MIX
Paper | Supporting
responsible forestry
FSC
www.fsc.org   FSC® C001695

INTRODUCTION
by Kev Carmody

Unbranded introduces us to that unique concept of oral historical storytelling in a written form. For tens of thousands of years humans have transmitted their cultures orally; the written form has been a late development in human evolution. Herb Wharton has masterly combined oral recollections and Indigenous cultural concepts into the written word.

The character Mulga takes the reader on an Indigenous cultural journey through cattle work, droving, cattle duffing and Indigenous (Murri) practices, including scrub running, rodeos, bush races and many more outback – as well as city – experiences. The divide between Murris who existed outside the Missions and those who were confined on Reserves is discussed by Mulga, who makes observations concerning education, politics, health, employment and many other aspects of our Murri culture that he feels should be addressed.

Unbranded points out the different attitudes towards the concept of Land Rights. The character Bindi perceives the land in a traditional way as a basis for spiritual and cultural strength, while others perceive the earth as an economic entity. Mulga describes the resilience of our Murri culture; an example of this is Bindi's wife who was traditionally chosen by the Elders as a 'proper wife'. The traditional way of existence was further severely challenged by the introduction of hard-hooved animals. Mulga's conclusion is that, in a myriad of ways, our Indigenous survival is based on 'adaptation' to the violent, colonial circumstances presented to us. The outback male mentality in reference to women is also touched upon by Mulga. Alcoholism was a constant theme of life for the majority of people in the country. The country pub was a magnet for most who worked in isolated jobs from daylight till dark, seven days a week. Mostly, the result of drinking was violence; this violence and alcoholism has led to unprecedented instances of incarceration, suicide, and cultural, societal and family disruption.

Herb states: 'it was [and is] a crime to be black'. The outback exhibits the rigid class and societal hierarchy of the Australian worker and the squattocracy. Jackaroos were aligned and lived with the managers and squattocracy, as opposed to the stockmen and other station workers. *Unbranded* also highlights the mechanisation of the grazing and farming sectors. This in turn forced an exodus of people from the country to the cities and towns. Herb pointedly describes Mulga's foray into the urban environment as 'alone among one thousand people', similar to what Henry Lawson described in his poem 'Faces in the Street'. The independence of droving and cattle work is contrasted against the sedentary labour of working to a set time in one place in the urban environment. Herb was writing *Unbranded* at a time of massive social transformation. Workers who voted for socialist-type governments became voters for country conservative candidates; over time, a third character, Sandy, becomes an example of this transformation as he eventually votes for the Country Party.

The great storytelling achievement of this book is the fact that Mulga's alter ego (Herb) is telling the stories from a lived experience. Readers can almost smell the mutton fat and linseed oil that was used to rub onto saddles, bridles and pack saddles to help preserve the leather. They can hear the clunking of the hobble chains and the ringing of the Condamine bells. The description of scrub running takes us into the realms of Banjo Paterson's poem 'The Man from Snowy River'. It was dangerous work yet, through all these cattle industry jobs, Mulga navigates easily because 'he believes in himself'. He was very confident because he had vast experience in all types of station work. He knew the jobs.

The travelling hawkers were another feature of the outback; R.M. Williams presented his merchandise in glossy catalogues with big photographs because people could not read or write, and so items were selected from the photographs. Canned goods started to have an impact on nomadic lives, providing more variety for outback meal-times, which were mainly damper and corned meat with spuds, onions and pumpkin. More significantly, strikes by Indigenous workers for better pay and conditions started to be carried out across Australia. The 1967 referendum that recognised us as people was part of this era. The impact that Maralinga atomic tests had on Australia, and on the Indigenous traditional custodians, has yet to be evaluated. Mulga is informed of all these important events through the 'bush telegraph' – last month's newspapers or the wireless. The descriptive portrayals of the Mt Isa Rodeo and the bush horseraces make readers feel as if they are standing in the ring watching the bookies betting odds, or getting ready to watch the competitor go down on the bareback horse in Chute No. 3. The underhand habits of some of the country race jockeys are so succinctly described I am sure I knew some of the same hoops (jockeys). Throughout this outback journey Mulga says laughter was a safety valve: a release from the hardness of outback life. He says, 'humour is a shield'; it was an intrinsic part of human existence.

Mulga's train travel over the Great Dividing Range is akin to his journey through life. Observing the past and the present with no regrets about the disappearance or passing of the 'Old Era'. Modernisation to Mulga had its distinctive positive elements. The legend of the 'Munta-gutta', however, connects Mulga back to the traditional stories before colonisation – a brotherhood connection with Bindi's ancient spiritual learning. The Old Peoples taught from the night-sky, utilising the blackboard of stars and galaxies that reflected countless stories from the

Dreaming, the repository or keeping place of wisdom, lore and identity. The spaces in between the stars and galaxies (the dark matter) were just as important in the stories. The account of the mystical 'min-min lights' that have been integrated into Australia's outback consciousness is described deftly by Mulga. Bindi's clan go on annual visits to the spiritual and cultural places where cultural and spiritual customs are performed with dance, stories and song. Mulga's transformation or transition from the Yumba to the towns is a description of our Indigenous interaction with the imposition of the European invasion. Our Indigenous culture is tens of thousands of years old.

The occurrence of droughts and floods are included in Mulga's recollections. The European occupation has been severely challenged by the unique weather patterns that Australia exhibits; as mentioned above, the introduced animal species were not bred initially for the Australian climate. Lack of water was one of the key determinants of the grazing industry's slow expansion. Mulga also states the vital importance of education for our Indigenous population. The progress towards advancement and equality cannot be contemplated without the basic ingredient of education. Mulga emphasises that all human societies will have to be included for homo sapiens to achieve fundamental inclusion into basic humanity.

Unbranded is a written documentary from an Indigenous oral perspective, making it a vital record of historical storytelling. Herb Wharton is a great storyteller, and this makes *Unbranded* a great book.

1

This is the story of three men. The dreams, the goals and the memories they shared. Their background beliefs and the colour of their skin were different, but never a bar to their friendship. They were the best of mates, each helping the other to achieve his ambition. They shared the past, planned the future, shaped their dreams, then made them happen.

As the sun set behind the red mulga hills, the clouds reflected colours of the rainbow: crimson, violet, gold, red. The hilltops and trees were silhouettes against the darkening sky. Two roos, their shapes outlined darkly, hopped along the ridge heading for the sweeter, greener grass that grew on the flats below, where surface water was everywhere, the gilgai full as the wet season came to an end.

At the foot of the hill a camp fire glowed and horses fed close by. No sound of horse bells, only the rattle or click of hobble chains. Two men sat around eating corn beef stew; a billy of tea stood close to the fire and the bedourie oven. Pack saddles and bags were stacked close by with the swags. Two bags near the fire held cooking and eating gear, a piece of calico spread out acted as a table. On it lay tea, sugar, salt and pepper, a bottle of hot sauce, a tin of golden syrup and a half-eaten damper, besides a few tin plates and knives, forks and spoons.

The men ate in silence after a hard day of chasing wild cattle, throwing some by the tail, dehorning and castrating them where they fell, always hunting them into the herd. For the last few weeks they had been gathering their herd of unbranded cattle, which was growing larger by the day: that was why there were no horse bells. Hearing them, cattle would move away. But another reason was that these men did not own the country or the cattle they mustered. The land was part of a pastoral empire owned by some rich absentee landlord who resided overseas. The men saw nothing wrong with helping themselves to the unbranded cattle that roamed in untold numbers on this vast, badly managed station known as Mulga Downs. They reasoned that they were doing the owners a favour if the owner could not manage and brand his herd; they were helping to control the herd and tame some of those unbranded cattle.

One of the men rose and walked to a tree where a night horse was tied. As the last bit of daylight faded he rode about fifty yards to where another man was riding around the outside of the yard, which was made from hessian about six feet high rolled out around the trees, used as posts. As the two met they talked for a while, then the short, stout white man rode back to the fire, leaving the tall Aboriginal man to watch the herd.

Sandy, the white man, washed in a shallow dish, then ate supper. Across the fire sat Bindi, another Aborigine. He was average height, slim, and wiry looking. He was silent as he stared into the flickering fire. This land was once Bindi's tribal land. For a moment he imagined he saw in the flames the image of a hundred tribal men as they danced long ago. Tomorrow, he thought, the coals and ash from the fire would cool, then like spirits of his tribal past the ash would scatter across the red brown land. He was one of the last of his tribe who practised tribal rites and knew the secrets handed down by word of mouth. He had no interest in who owned and branded the alien white man's meat. His only feeling was for the land itself. To get back some of his tribal land was his dream and to pass on to his sons a culture almost lost, the legends from the Dreamtime past.

Across the fire Sandy was also deep in thought, recalling his father's years of toil to save and buy the small block of land that was now called Red Hills Station. For years he struggled, droving to help get the station started, then died of a heart attack, leaving Sandy – his only son – to carry on. Sandy's mother had died when he was a boy and he was raised by an aunt, until his father took him droving or mustering. Now he was the owner of Red Hills and he had his own dream. He thought of his father's years toiling for the big overseas owned stations.

Sandy did not want to be neighbour to the big stations, he wanted to have his own cattle empire. He concentrated his thoughts on the herd of cattle held behind the hessian yard. Here on Mulga Downs country they were miles from home. It was unlikely they would see anyone as the roads were impassable and packhorses were never used on Mulga Downs. The men had worked on Mulga Downs before as stockmen and knew the country. They had planned the muster well in advance, waited till the time was ripe. The task was almost over. If they were caught now Sandy would be finished. If they succeeded he would be on his way to his cattle empire. For weeks they had mustered in what they jokingly called their 'back paddock'. Working from dawn till dusk, taking turns at night watch. All day chasing and throwing cattle, galloping after fresh mobs, shouldering them into the herd, changing horses sometimes four times a day. Never relaxing, always on the alert, cattle always trying to break away from the herd. Sleeping in swags, living hard, they kept going. Now they were almost finished.

The three men had one thing in common. All had a strong dislike of the manager of Mulga Downs, a mean old red-faced bastard who seemed to know nothing of cattle or how to manage the millions of acres he ruled from the safety of the verandah, where he sat and sipped his whisky. Never leaving the comfort of the big old homestead, he skimped and short-changed the stockmen he employed. Anyone could get a job here, men never stayed long because of the conditions and the tucker – or lack of it. That was why the manager was nicknamed 'Sugar-Bag'. Even when mustering was in full swing and men wanted more food out in the mustering camp, he would never send out more than could be put in a sugar bag. One time when the men complained about having no vegetables, he said, 'Okay, I'll send some out.' Next day a jackaroo turned up with a sugar bag. In the bottom of the bag were three potatoes, two onions and a packet of Dewcrisp to last eight men two weeks.

Nowadays Mulga Downs was rundown because of the cheap labour Sugar-Bag employed, mostly jackaroos from the upper-crust mob. 'Marsupials', they were referred to by the stockmen whose bosses they would become. Ability meant little on the big stations. If you didn't attend private school you would be a stockman until you died, especially if you were an Aborigine, no matter what knowledge you had of the land or stock. This was why Bindi and Mulga had decided to help Sandy duff the mob of unbranded cattle from the vast unfenced acres of Mulga Downs. Now they were almost ready to head back to Red Hills and stamp its brand on these cleanskins.

Sandy finished eating, then spoke to Bindi about the day's muster. They estimated they had four hundred head now. They spoke of the weather. Would it be best to head for home tomorrow? Rain seemed to be getting closer and if it did rain heavily then all traces of their tracks would be washed out. Not that jackaroos would be likely to notice anything amiss when they mustered here later in the year.

Soon they stoked up the night log on the fire and crawled into their swags. The night was warm. From the gilgai came the croak of frogs and the sound of crickets and a thousand other insects. Mosquitoes whined. A plover called; from far away came the lone, mournful howl of a dingo. Sometimes, riding around the herd, Mulga broke into a curse or a song to let the cattle know he was there. If he remained silent he might frighten the sleeping cattle; they might wake and see the mute figure riding by. That was one way to start a cattle rush or stampede, as the Yanks would say.

Mulga, unlike his full-blood cousin Bindi on his mother's side, or Sandy, who was related to him on his father's side, held no ambition of winning a cattle empire or regaining his tribal land. The world was his kingdom. He had been reared in one of the camps or yumbas that used to exist on the fringe of western towns, where the Murris lived in tents or shacks made from saplings, tin and bags. To Mulga, his independence was worth all the empires. In the yumbas, for years men and women had fought for equal rights and education. They had escaped the church-run missions, the tea and sugar handouts of government rations. They worked on the stations, laboured on the roads, in shearing sheds, along the railway lines. They still hunted the tribal meat sometimes, and some still listened to the stories of the old people – legends handed down by word of mouth. Meanwhile, the kids were sent to the white man's school to learn his legends.

Mulga's father had instilled in his son the importance of all sorts of learning. The first thing Mulga learned about in school was prejudice, which was also rife in the township. During those early days in school he soon learned to run fast or stand and fight. He also learned what interested him most and realised early on that ignorant people were the biggest racists and usually the dumbest folk around.

At school he could beat most of the others at their own games. He beat them in exams, even though he played the wag a lot. Yet he realised early in life he would have to fight for anything he sought. The only things Mulga sought were some answers and independence. He soon found that even the history books did not tell the true history of the land. At school he learned of the discovery of this great land by white sailors. A wide uncharted unmapped land. At night he listened to the tales around the smoky fires. How the birds and animals came to be. The stories told in stars, rivers, hills and sky. These stories not in the history book told how the land was charted, mapped and known to a race of people for thousands of years, their footprints stamped upon the ground for all to see, like roadways. Fifty thousand years of footprints were stamped upon the earth long before white explorers came or white settlers followed.

Quite early in life Mulga realised that not everything he read and heard was true. The history books told of massacres of a handful of settlers by the so-called ignorant savage black. But they did not tell why the black man fought back. They did not tell of the wholesale murder of thousands of men, women and children by the ignorant savage white tribes in their quest for land rights. This history Mulga learned at night around camp fires. He learned, for instance, about the forced removals of the elders to the mission stations. Of the slave conditions on some stations, the pittance paid to some workers.

Mulga left home young to go droving. Since then he had roamed the outback working at all sorts of jobs, mostly stockwork. He fought for better wages and conditions on the stations for both black and white. Equal rights and education for his own people was his call. Although he had a deep feeling for the land, he believed no tribe, clan or religious creed owned any patent on the earth. The earth belonged to all. To Mulga, the soil itself was sacred. All life came from the earth and when people died they returned to it. All life depended on it.

As Mulga came to understand the white written history, then learned of the unwritten black history of Australia, it seemed that everything went wrong for the Murri about 150 years ago. Too many white criminals were imported to Paradise, where they built gaols. Later, their leg irons undone, those criminals shot, poisoned or gaoled the Murris, were granted land rights and became the white oppressors – they who had been the oppressed. Today, it was the blacks who were calling for land rights. Could the oppressed blacks become the black oppressors of tomorrow? No, it was not in their nature. Australia was too small a country for divisions of any kind. Education, Mulga thought, was the key to everything. He dreamed of a standard legal and education system regardless of state borders or religious beliefs. Surely it was possible for everyone to enjoy a similar lifestyle and still have different beliefs.

Now, as Mulga rode round the herd, he saw no crime in mustering cattle neglected by the men on whose country they ran. For years station workers were not paid what they were worth. In the law courts station owners had argued that being a good stockman was not a trade, so that they could go on paying the same wage to every employee. The squatter always opposed wage rises, claiming that being a good stockman was unskilled work. Managers like Sugar-Bag and the men he represented Mulga held in contempt. He worked for them and did his job to the best of his ability. He owed no allegiances to such men, although he had met and worked for bosses he liked and respected. He took delight in helping Sandy take cattle from men like Sugar-Bag, who would never get their hands or clothes dirty. The owners raped the land, taking all the profits overseas. When the land was flogged bare and over-stocked they screamed for government handouts or else moved on, investing in something else.

Mulga also wanted to see some justice, the demise of an oppressive government ruled mainly by these who represented the graziers' empires. The graziers ruled like feudal lords and controlled the local shire councils. It took only fifty votes to elect one of these squatters, yet in the towns it took one thousand votes to elect someone to the council. These men were a law unto themselves.

Mulga realised that money was everything. Principles seemed to matter little if you were a member of the ruling squatter class, the oppressive government or the police force. Mulga wondered how some of these men could take oaths to uphold the law and the integrity of society. He also noted with disgust decisions made by judges and magistrates clearly biased against the Murri. He wondered how so much value could be placed upon the book upon which the white man swore his oath of truth and honesty: to him it made a mockery of justice. He thought that men should be made to swear on something more substantial than a book. Maybe they should stake their wealth, then: integrity or life itself.

As Mulga rode around the hessian yard most of the cattle settled for the night. He looked up into the night sky, and now his thoughts went far beyond cattle empires and governments. Mulga was fascinated by space, the vastness of the universe. By comparison the earth seemed insignificant like a grain of sand in the desert. Already he had seen a man walk on the moon: now his ambition was to witness a flight to the stars. His ambition went beyond Sandy's cattle empire or Bindi's territorial boundaries.

At ten o'clock he woke Bindi and handed him his pocket watch. Bindi would wake Sandy at one o'clock. In the daylight hours they did not need a watch; they started work before the sun rose and finished after it had set. Lunch time was when they had time off and the cattle rested.

2

Next morning at four o'clock Sandy woke the other two sleeping men. Bindi reheated the stew, turned it into a curry and cooked some johnny-cakes on the coals and ash, while Mulga unhobbled the horses and bought them back to camp. Catching his day horse and pack animals, he tied them to the trees. Bindi finished eating, rolled his swag, caught his horse and relieved Sandy, who turned the hungry night horse free to eat.

As Sandy and Mulga sat eating by the fire they talked of the day ahead. Should they head for home now they had plenty of cattle? In the north heavy clouds were building up: even as they ate a few spits of rain came down. They decided they would head for home. For the last few weeks they had mustered around in a huge circle and were now only about twelve miles from Red Hills Station. The men finished eating, rolled their swags, filled the pack bags. Then, saddling up, they rode to the herd, leaving the packhorses tied to trees.

The big bank of clouds grew darker in the northern sky as the men opened up the yard and let the cattle out.

With whips and curses they steadied the lead, keeping the beasts from rushing off. After they were settled Mulga quickly undid the hessian yard and rolled it into bundles. He walked the packhorses to the rolls of hessian, and threw them on top of the pack bags, securing them with a surcingle and cross straps. Then, gathering the horses, he headed them in the direction of Red Hills.

The horses needed no steering: heads turned for home in the greyish light. Rain began to fall. With the horses leading the cattle followed, the three men chasing wayward beasts back into the mob. Some horses, impatient to be home, began to trot. Sandy rode in the lead to steady them while Bindi and Mulga worked and cursed the mob as the rain became a steady drizzle. As they headed home they picked up a few extra cleanskins but did not look too hard for more. The sun was now hidden behind the clouds and as the rain became heavier the cattle were easier to control. Heads down they followed the horses, seeking safety from men and rain among the herd. They reached the boundary fence. The ground was squashy underfoot as they opened the barbed wire fence in a stony creek that was now a few inches deep with red muddy water. As the cattle walked up the creek bed, all trace of their tracks was washed out where they went through the fence. The rain was now a steady downpour. Between two hills they stopped to change horses and rest the cattle. Nothing seemed to move in the whitish wet shroud-like landscape except a big old roo that stood up and gazed down but did not leave the safety of a cave just below the crumbling rocky hilltop. Horses and cattle, heads bowed, stood silent as the rain continued to fall.

From there on the trip home was easy going. The men reached their home yard in pouring rain and the cattle followed the horses straight inside. They led the packhorse to the garage-like shed that was their house, stowed the packs inside, placed some horses in a small paddock and turned the rest loose. Water now lay everywhere as the old packhorses were relieved of their burdens and turned loose, unhobbled for the first time in weeks. They sought relief from their itching backs by rolling in the soft wet mud. Then, shaking themselves, they trotted off down the paddock to a well earned rest.

Inside, the men busied themselves lighting a fire in the old wood stove in one corner of the huge shed, a recess cut out and enclosed with tin. A chimney poked up through the roof. Outside, Bindi was splitting pieces from the woodstack and carrying them inside. An enormous black cast iron kettle stood on the stove. Sandy filled it from a tap that protruded from the wall. The water came from the big rainwater tank on the side of the shed. Close to the stove hung saucepans and frying pans, and along one wall ran planks of timber stacked with bottles of sauce, honey, pickles, tins of meat, fruit, treacle, milk, coffee and other things. Beneath were drums of flour, tea and sugar, dried fruits, rice, custard powder and foods in packets, well protected from the rats and mice and the weather.

Away from the wall stood an old table and around it were grouped half a dozen four gallon drums. From the rafters hung a Tilley lamp. There was a big kerosene fridge. As Sandy heated a meal of tinned curry and Bindi split the wood, Mulga busied himself cleaning the fridge inside and out and filled it from a drum of kero. Tomorrow they would be able to store fresh meat. With a yard full of cattle and the fridge going, they would have fresh meat tonight.

They sat down at the table and realised that this was the first time in weeks they could relax. They felt relief and a sense of achievement. They had set out to do a hard and dangerous job. Day and night they had had to guard their herd. Now they could laugh and joke. The cattle were safe behind a six-foot wooden fence. They discussed what had to be done. They finally decided to draft the Mulga Downs branded cattle from the mob and take them back through the fence. Holding them here was dangerous; they could not sell them and they would only eat Red Hills grass. Besides, if it kept raining there would be no tracks coming or going to Mulga Downs. By tomorrow they would have only their own cattle on Red Hills.

After a short rest the men walked to the cattle yards and forced the mob into smaller yards. As Bindi and Mulga worked the gates Sandy drafted the cattle through the yards. Occasionally a micky bull or some old cantankerous cow charged, but the rest of the cattle followed the leaders through the drafting yard.

In no time they had finished. About eighty branded cattle were drafted off. Bindi and Sandy caught horses from the paddock and as Mulga opened the gate to let them go they rushed from the yard, heading home. The men steadied the lead for a while as some old cows on the tail, their cleanskin calves still in the yard, wanted to stay, but a good flogging with a whip got them moving. Bindi went with Sandy for a couple of miles then returned to help Mulga kill their meat.

Gathering knives and bags, they drove the Land Rover to the yard, through wet slushy ground. The rain had now eased to a steady shower. They drafted off a branded Mulga Downs cow then shot her and swiftly began to skin and bone the carcass where it lay, cutting steaks, roasts and chunks of brisket to be salted. As blood sometimes upset the cattle, later they would return to move the skin and offal. On a sandy ridge at the back of the shed stood the meathouse, a small, single gauzed-in room with a high tin roof to catch the breeze. Inside, two pipes ran from wall to wall and from them hung steel and wire hooks. A bench ran along one wall with a round chopping block cut from a gydgea tree. As the men hung up the fresh meat, Bindi began salting the meat to be corned, cutting long deep slashes in the flesh, rubbing in salt, then stacking it in a heap.

With a bag of fresh meat and rib-bones Mulga headed for the kitchen while Bindi started the Land Rover and drove back to the yard to move the remains of the carcass. Meanwhile, Mulga cooked their first meal of fresh meat for almost two weeks. Bindi returned and, gathering dry clothes, headed to the shed, which acted as a wash-and-bath-house. He had a shower in the big galvanised iron tubs, with the bucket of water on the pulley rope above. In the kitchen Mulga had potatoes and pumpkin boiling alongside sizzling steaks. After Mulga had showered they sat around to wait for Sandy, so they could all enjoy their first decent meal in days. As they waited they ate juicy rib-bones cooked on top of the stove.

When Sandy returned it was almost dark; the Tilley lamp was burning brightly. After he had cleaned up they sat down to what they considered a feast: steak, potatoes, pumpkin and gravy. As they sat around their table, the drums they used as chairs felt like thrones and the strong black tea they drank from enamel mugs could have been champagne in crystal glasses. They joked and laughed about the hard times of a few days ago. The buster Bindi had, the charging cleanskins, the near misses and close shaves that could have been fatal. They could laugh at these things now the tension had lifted; now they could relax. The cattle were safe, the rain would leave no evidence. Mulga suggested they should send old Sugar-Bag a bill with all the hours of overtime they had spent mustering his cattle, eighteen hours a day for weeks. They swore again they had done Sugar-Bag a favour by mustering his country and branding all the cattle for him – even if it was the Red Hills brand they used. They decided to wait to see what the daylight would bring. If it was fine they would brand, castrate and earmark the cattle. Happy, contented and tired, they went to bed.

★

Next morning the rain had ceased. Empty clouds drifted south pushed by the fresh morning breeze. They cooked more steak and gravy and began sorting the meat, filling the fridge with steak and roasts, putting the salted meat into bags, which they hung up to be cured by the brine. As the sun tried to break through the clouds they headed for the yard. Most of the unbranded cattle were too big to scruff, so they decided to brand them all in the cattle crush. They started a fire in a hollow log. A slot cut near the top held the branding irons, the handle resting on a wire between two pegs to keep them from falling out of the fire. As the flames rushed up the inside of the hollow log, with the branding irons catching all the heat, the fire fed on the dry inside of the log. No need to stoke it or chop wood all the time. So they sharpened pocket knives, checked dehorners and earmarking pliers as they waited for the brands to heat.

Then the job of branding, castrating and earmarking began as they stood in the packed crush. Bindi stamped on the brand irons, now red-hot, while Mulga earmarked and Sandy, reaching through the rails, grabbed the balls of a cleanskin bull. With a couple of swift nicks and slashes of his pocket-knife he desexed them before they realised what had happened. As the cattle came through they fought and struggled in the crush, sometimes charging in the forcing pens.

Steadily they toiled all morning. As the sun rose higher it became hot and humid. Broken clouds still hung around. The ground, wet and squashy before, became boggy and sticky. As the men climbed the rails of the crush to dehorn the cattle or earmark they began to sweat and curse. Once they stopped for five minutes for a smoke and a drink of water, another time the log burnt out and they replaced it from a stack heaped against the yard. By midday they decided to rest. They had laboured for six hours and decided they had more than half the herd branded, so they headed to the shed for a meal and a rest.

Looking beyond the yards they saw small puddles of water everywhere in the creek, while along the horse paddock fence the small red claypan was like a miniature lake. As the sun shone down it glistened and sparkled around the edges. A flock of cackling galahs flew down to the water, a magpie chortled from near the windmill and around the carcass of last night's kill. A hawk and some crows fought and cawed and whistled as they feasted. In the sky they fought each other; circling high they would come swooping down upon another bird as it tried to make off with the spoils. As the men watched, waiting for their own steaks to cook, they were reminded of the aerial battle scenes they had seen in war movies. Only here it was no dog fight in the sky: it was a bird fight. They soared high above, gliding round and round then with wings folded back they came swooping down like dive bombers on their enemy – any bird that had a piece of meat, no matter if it was the same species. Out here nature's law was survival of the fittest.

The men, tired, hungry and muddy, ate their meal, then rested for a short while. They returned to the yard, lit a fire and were soon toiling steadily again. Filling the crush, emptying it, then hunting up the cattle until at last they knew that only one last crushful of cattle remained. The last lot was forced in and christened with the brand of Red Hills Station, and as the last beast left the crush the three men gave a mighty cheer, their task almost complete. All the cattle were safely mustered, yarded and branded. With about two hours of daylight left they saddled up and let the now almost starving cattle walk out of the yard to the grassy flats where they dropped their heads to eat hungrily. Mulga returned to camp to cook more steak and potatoes while Sandy and Bindi headed the cattle into a holding paddock. Just before sundown they rode home.

That night, clean and full of more fresh meat, the three men sat around the table. The only remaining thing to do was to scatter the freshly branded cattle through the Red Hills herd.

In a few months' time no-one would know where these cattle came from. The only thing that mattered now was that they wore the Red Hills brand.

Mulga and Bindi did not work for Sandy full-time. They helped him with mustering, fencing, droving and many other small jobs, coming and going as they pleased when they were not employed by other stations. They would come to Red Hills to rest and break-in horses. Weeks ago when they had left town with Sandy they told people they were going to fence and repair yards. They had planned the muster well in advance. The rain that came in the last few days was a bonus: everything had gone right for them. They would now be paid so much a head for the cattle they had branded.

As they sat around the table drinking tea they tallied up their wages. They had cleaned up almost four hundred head of unbranded cattle for old Sugar-Bag from his unmanageable herd. They reasoned it would be much easier for Mulga Downs to muster now that they had lightened the herd. To Mulga, Bindi and Sandy, cattle running wild and unbranded belonged to those who could catch and brand them. The three men discussed the pay. Sandy added up three weeks' wages for the men for 'fencing'. This he would pay by cheque in case of any trouble and note it in his account books. When they reached town he would pay them the balance in cash. It was Sandy who stood to gain most in the future. The longer he held the cattle, the bigger and fatter they would grow and the more money they would bring. He had agreed to pay Bindi and Mulga four pounds each for every cleanskin they gathered: sixteen hundred pounds.

Bindi, always careful with money, had already spent some of his pay buying horses from Sandy, as well as an old ute. Mulga, as always, decided he would spend his money on a trip to the city, on booze, women and racehorses. As soon as the roads dried out, he would head south for a few months. Sandy talked about building a house with a huge verandah; one day he would marry and raise his kids here. Bindi had the same plan to marry and raise his kids on his tribal land, part of which lay on Red Hills. But to Mulga women were like the cheques he earned: hard to get and easy to lose.

3

Next day the sun rose bright and hot and with it came the flies. The three men ate breakfast then rode out to muster. The cattle, still wayward, had to be flogged back into the herd then held around the water trough for a while. Then the men returned to the shed to spend the day cleaning up and washing clothes.

Bindi, sweeping dirt away, told Mulga: 'Someday I'll own some land again like my tribal ancestors.' Sandy, as he tried to clean up his dingy little office, said: 'One day I'll own a great big station with a huge office and plenty of room.' And Mulga, straightening up the books and papers that always seemed to litter the floor around his bed, said aloud: 'One day I'll buy a bloody bookcase for myself and a big desk, then sit down and write a bloody book about the things I've seen.' They had said these things to each other many times before, maybe in jest, maybe in hope.

A roast cooked slowly in the wood stove. The day grew hotter; already most of the puddles had evaporated in the heat. The hawks and crows still fought over the carcass now picked almost bare by the birds, ants and dingoes. A steady stream of water spurted from the pipe of the pumping windmill into an overflowing water tank. The water ran down a small gully to a waterhole in the creek, just through the fence of the holding paddock where a few cattle camped under the trees. As the sun set the men sat down to a meal of roast beef and talked late into the night about the droving trips ahead later in the year. Tomorrow they would rise early and take the cattle to the rock hole, turn them loose then wait for the road to dry. Then it was off to town and wine, women and song.

Next day their job was fully completed. They swung their horses' heads for home, all evidence washed away by the rain. The cattle would soon scatter, grass was growing high and green everywhere, they would look after themselves. Even the horses seem to sense relief now the task was finished: headed for home, their step grew brisk. The men, lighthearted, proud of a job well done, let them gallop the last mile back.

Three days later, spent greasing leather, making tools and waiting impatiently for the roads to dry out, the three men packed the Land Rover with swags and ports. They emptied the fridge and packed the bags with fresh and salted meat, then headed off for town. They followed the narrow bush track that led to Mulga Downs, through the bush they knew so well. Sticking to the hard higher ground, they reached the station without much trouble. When they pulled up at the office a bookkeeper and some jackaroos came out, followed by old Sugar-Bag, with his vast belly, and pale face. He told them the road to town was okay, he had been over it yesterday. They were given some mail to post then headed off.

Now the road was a built-up dirt highway. Arriving in town, they got rid of Sugar-Bag's mail, then headed to where Sandy stayed with his aunt. They left some meat there and the rest they dropped down to the Murris' camp, where Bindi and Mulga sometimes stayed with their mates.

Their next stop was the pub, where they were greeted by some old mates and others wanting drinks. In the lounge sat the usual mob of lounge lizards, calling loudly when they saw the three men walk in, knowing they had just finished work and would be good for a party. The publican's wife gave them a warm welcome; she knew they would spend up big for a few days, especially Mulga. They ordered beers and shouted for their mates, and Bindi and Mulga both cashed their pay cheques. A new blonde barmaid served them. Most of the country hotels seemed to want to employ the prettiest barmaids, so they came and went all the time.

Mulga had left his swag with a mate called Jack, a Murri from Mulga's country. They had worked together many times and had many binges together over the years. Jack had married and now had five kids. Molly, his wife, who never drank, was like a sister to Bindi and Mulga.

She never seemed to complain and always had a meal ready when Jack and his mates arrived home half-pissed. Now Jack came into the pub and joined in the drinking. After a few beers, Bindi, Mulga and Jack, feeling hungry, asked Sandy to drive them home. Sandy pulled up at Molly and Jack's house and let them off, then headed off on his own business.

The house that Molly and Jack lived in was made from sheets of unpainted tin of different shapes. A few more pieces partitioned off the kitchen from a couple of bedrooms. The kitchen furnishings were sparse: a wood stove, a big table, a few rickety chairs, a kerosene fridge, and a dresser with shelves covered with newspaper, the edges snipped with scissors to make a pattern. Here they would all sit and talk for hours, over a supply of beer or a pot of tea. Outside was a bough shed where they usually slept, with four or five stretchers scattered around. Nearby was the bathroom, constructed from more sheets of tin, with a dark blanket hung between two saplings to act as a door. It had an old-fashioned tub, chipped and water-stained. Two big washtubs stood outside the bathroom, next to the water tap that served four houses. The toilet was a hole dug in the ground with a thunder-box placed on top, smelling of disinfectant.

Within a few minutes of Bindi and Mulga's arrival, more Murris gathered at the house. Their first words always seemed to be, not 'Good-day' but 'You got a smoke?' Murris never seemed to have smokes. They were a happy lot, all the same, with the knack of being able to survive thanks to their sense of humour, even in the midst of tragedy. Most had suffered major misfortune, but they would shrug it off with a joke about themselves and their woes. Imagine the uproar, Mulga thought, if whites had to endure the hardships and prejudice the Murris faced every day. Even when they fought among themselves, ten minutes later they would be mates again. These were the fringe-dwellers of the western towns whose struggle, Mulga believed, was harder than most of those who lived in the third world. Slave wages for most. Nothing handed out to them. They struggled for everything they got and received continual harassment and abuse from the police.

This was the world that Jack, Mulga and Bindi inhabited. They had mates who were white, some whom they respected, and they had even known some good policemen. But as they talked together about their problems, they realised that Australia was a white-dominated racist country that would not acknowledge its black past. They saw the advances made by Murris and knew that change would come only through education and the mutual understanding of both white and black. These concerns, as well as the wages paid to every station worker, came to the fore when they bailed up at the stations for fair deals. The misguided swell-headed squatter would brand them troublemakers, but this meant nothing to them. Their independence lay in being able to say what they wanted to whoever they liked. They would call no man 'master'. Sometimes this attitude led to fights in the town and on the stations. It was remarkable how many people did not like to hear the truth about themselves. Mulga had noted that those fringe-dwellers who did not rush to thank the ignorant station bosses who chucked them worthless scraps were also labelled troublemakers. But these Murris did not want scraps. Scraps were for the ants.

After a meal of cold meat and salads they lay down for a few hours' rest then made off to the 'Murris' pub' as it was called – they had one in every outback town where there was more than one hotel. As they left, Jack's three school kids and the two younger ones put in their orders to Bindi and Mulga for footballs and the like, and they gave Molly money to take the kids to the picture show, the only entertainment in town.

It was sundown as the men returned to the crowded hotel. The hotel lounge was packed with ringers from the stations, shearers, railway and council workers, white and black, and women out for a good time. There was a mixture of women of all colours, their classic nicknames fitting their status. Lady Mary, named for the airs she bunged on, sat at a table with Goolbury – named for her long brown scaly legs. Bicycle Kate, a blue-eyed blonde, was named for obvious reasons. Electric Lill was a small, quiet woman who once lit up the whole town. But the favourite among the drovers was the big-breasted brunette known as the Night-Mare. It was claimed that after dark, like all good night horses, any drover could mount her. This was the pub on Friday night: willing women, randy bushmen, plenty of grog and always some fights, sometimes between men, sometimes between women.

As the beer flowed and the crowd grew noisier, Bindi and Mulga, both singled out by old girls they knew, drank and shouted like most bushmen when they had money. The women were now calling them 'darling', and to the stockmen with each drink they took the women looked more beautiful. By closing time the men, fresh from the bush and now half-pissed, bought cartons of beer and bottles of wine and rum and with an assorted mob headed for a favourite drinking spot a few miles from the town. With a fire alight they drank and loved the night away out of sight and sound of town.

When Mulga woke at daylight all was quiet. He lay on a piece of calico with the Night-Mare. He got up to stoke the fire and looked around him. In the dim light lay many bodies, some sleeping in cars, others still in tight embrace on the ground. A half-full bottle of rum stood near the fire with a carton of beer. Mulga began to shout to everyone telling them it was time to be up.

The only answer he got was abuse. 'Get back to sleep ya bastard!' 'Go and catch the horses, you bastard! You've got the bloody Night-Mare tied up!' Soon, however, Mulga was joined by Bindi and a few others. They sat around feeling seedy, sucking on a stubbie or taking swigs of rum from the bottle, until at last everyone awoke, finished off the rest of the grog, then headed back to town.

Bindi and Mulga shaved and showered at Jack's place. Mulga had decided to leave. He would have to book a seat on the old DC3, the weekly airmail service to the city. Before they were ready to leave Sandy arrived and asked how they had spent the night. As they talked he told Mulga and Bindi he had their money for them. Mulga decided to leave most of his with Sandy till he boarded the plane. But he would need some for today – on Saturdays he liked to bet with the S.P. Bookies, and he had to shout Molly and Jack. Sandy pulled a roll of notes from his pocket and handed them both four hundred quid.

Sandy drove Mulga and Bindi straight off to the R.M. Williams shop to do their shopping and buy up big. In every western town there was an R.M. Williams establishment where stockmen could buy anything: saddles, packs, knives, rope – some even claimed they had bought droving plants there. Then, after booking a seat on the plane, the men returned to the pub.

Mulga, a racing form in his hand, searched for winners while Bindi, still with Bicycle hanging on to him, sipped beer and talked to Sandy. The S.P. shop was a billiards room where the dice game was played sometimes on weekends. Picking out a couple of horses, Mulga placed his bets then settled down to drink.

In any pub there was always someone broke, and to these men they would always give money, never lend. Mulga and Bindi had been broke many times themselves, and it seemed to be some sort of stockman's code to help each other, no matter the colour of your skin. So they passed the day, Mulga busy punting. In the evening he rested, listening to the races on the big old valve radio of Jack's that seemed to crackle with static especially when a race came on. Mulga had a good day winning on the races, and that night they returned to the pub, to more beer and arguments, wine and women. Then another big party and the next morning the same bodies and bottles scattered around the fire. After the 'heart-starter', as the first drink after the night before was called, they headed home.

Now Mulga's port was packed and his swag rolled, ready for the flight south. Soon Sandy came to take him to the aerodrome, a level graded strip of claypan ground about two miles from town. As they waited, Sandy handed Mulga the rest of his poddy-dodging money in cash. The old DC3 pulled up and Mulga boarded the plane, feeling the aircraft shudder as it got ready for take-off. Then they were racing along the dusty runway: as Mulga looked out of the window, dust rose up from behind the wing. The wind socket, looking like a worn out condom, flashed past then they rose. The treetops became smaller as they circled and he looked down on the cluster of glaring, shimmering, iron-roofed houses and shacks and wide dusty streets. Then it was all gone. There was only the empty sky and the drone of engines as Mulga headed for the city.

4

In the bright lights of the city Mulga soon squandered his hard-earned cheque, while Sandy and Bindi went on toiling outback. For a while Mulga thought he would work and live in the city, where every morning he watched the crowds swarming like ants out of the railway carriages, rushing to beat a factory siren or some other deadline. But after a few months he decided this life was not for him. On weekends the brightly lit hotel bar, the painted women; on weekdays the rush to work, always watching the clock. It seemed to Mulga that everything in the city was governed by the clock, with the workers always looking out apprehensively for the boss. How unlike the bush, where if someone saw the boss coming, they would sit down and wait for him to arrive and have a yarn with him. Here in the city, the men sat down most of the time, and as soon as the boss came into view they would spring to their feet and begin to look busy.

So Mulga greased his swag straps, packed his port and headed outback once more. And it was soon after his return to the bush, after he'd met up again with Sandy and Bindi and joined them on a big droving trip that they became the owners of an orphaned foal, destined to become known throughout the land as 'Comet'.

They had taken a mob of cattle from Black Rock Station down south. After months on the road, Mulga was left to take the horses back north. During the droving trip, one roan mare, a box-headed dumper type, had given birth to a foal, which was now about three months old. One morning, as Mulga drove the horses along the stock route, in a sheep station paddock owned by a well known sheep breeder and racehorse owner, he came upon a mare lying on the ground. She was dead, probably bitten by a snake. A foal, a colt, wheeled and whinnied around her body. Mulga inspected the dead mare: plainly one of the thoroughbred brood mares owned by the wealthy cocky. Eventually the foal joined the plant horses, now feeding beside a windmill. As Mulga boiled the billy, he watched the tall, clean-legged, racy looking foal mingle with the herd and start playing with old Roaney's foal. After a while her foal became thirsty and began to suck his mother's milk. Then a strange thing happened. The other foal, hungry after a couple of days without milk, tried to suck the roan mare. At first she aimed a couple of cow-kicks at the strange foal. Then, as Mulga watched, she let both foals drink her milk. The hungry new foal drank greedily, sometimes being kicked or nuzzled away by the mare, but he satisfied his thirst.

Well, Mulga mused to himself, it looks like we got ourselves a racehorse! The colt was a rich red bay foal with a star on his forehead. Mulga, resting on his swag, stared up at the spinning blades of the windmill and noticed the trademark in large black letters: COMET. Then he looked at the foal again and said to himself: 'I'll call him 'Comet'.' So the foal was named after a windmill on a lonely outback stock route.

Mulga stayed most of the day around the windmill, then packed up the horses and headed north again. The new foal had by now been firmly adopted by the roan mare and the other foal. That evening, just on sundown, Mulga reached the boundary gate of the big sheep station. With the wire fence now behind him, there was no chance of the foal going back to its dead mother.

When Mulga returned to Red Hills with the horses, they branded the foals before turning them loose in the spell paddock. They decided to leave Comet a stallion. (The other foal was never named but always known simply as 'Roaney's foal'.) Later, they discovered that the station where Comet was found was the home of some very famous racehorses whose owner was noted for the big bets he placed at outback race meetings. Years later, when Comet started to win races, there was much speculation about his breeding and where he came from. Sandy once tried to register the horse, but when he was asked about Comet's breeding, the only information he could give was: 'Sire and dam by the roadside – out of the paddock.' This was rejected by the racing officials, so Comet remained unregistered.

From the start Comet seemed to be something special. Learning easily to turn and gallop when chasing cattle, they soon realised how fast he was. Quiet-natured, he became a pet, but from the moment he was broken in and saddled he showed his spirit, throwing Mulga as he bucked around the yard. But he would buck only when he was fresh; as they later discovered, once in hand he was like a kids' pony: they would ride him bareback, slide off over his rump or crawl under his belly without a single kick aimed at them.

When Comet was almost four years old he was prepared for his first race at the big Mulga Downs picnic races, where the big stations from miles around brought their horses to try for the Mulga Cup. The three friends sat around the old table at Red Hills and planned their strategy. Mulga, just back from one of his wandering trips, and Bindi, over from Blackwater, were helping Sandy break in horses and get things together for the droving season ahead. Sometimes Sandy had two droving plants going, with either Bindi or Mulga in charge of one mob while he ran the other.

They decided they would take Comet on a droving trip and that Mulga would train him. Mulga had told them of an episode from his childhood days, how he was paid two bob a week as a stable hand, cleaning out the stalls, raking horse shit, feeding, watering and excercising the horses before and after school. Now those long dirty hours in the stables years ago were going to pay dividends for Mulga and his mates. Once again he told them about the trainer he'd worked for, a wily old bloke who seemed to know every trick in the book – and a lot more of his own. He was a past master at getting horses fit and patching up broken-down animals. And he knew how to make them win or lose. But even this wily old trainer sometimes came unstuck with his well laid plans and betting plunges, for nothing is a certainty in the racing game. He always seemed to be in trouble with racing officials, who would sometimes insist on swabbing his horses, whether they lost or won. The trainer would be most helpful about this, and after the races were over he would shout the stewards drinks before they headed off to the city with the swabs. But in the meantime, the trainer's mates would be busy removing all the swabs from the official car, then throwing them away in the rubbish dump or waterholes, stuffing them into a hollow log or down a rabbit burrow.

Some of the big betting squatters wagered thousands on their horses. Mulga told his mates how even the wily old trainer could sometimes catch himself and do his money. Mulga remembered one time strapping a horse on race day. The horse had won this big race four times before, but was now replaced by a younger stable star. It was a one mile race. As the horses were led into the saddling paddock before legging up the jockeys, the old trainer told his young, inexperienced jockey just to let the old horse drop out. 'Don't knock him around, he's got no chance,' he told him. Then, to the other jockey on his stable star, he said: 'You're on a certainty, he couldn't be beat.' Watching with interest and studying the horses as they paraded was the racing official from whose car the swabs had disappeared while he drank with the old trainer. He remarked to another official how well the old horse looked, and as the horses headed onto the track he handed him forty quid. 'Put this on the old horse,' he said. He had smelt something wrong.

As the bookies called the odds the old horse was 33-1 and the other, the stable star, was being backed for a fortune: his price was even money and getting shorter. The official headed for the barrier as the horses milled around before the start. He told all the jockeys he would be watching them; if they did not ride a clean race he would rub them out. Then he walked up to the young jockey on the old horse and told him how to ride the race. He told the kid, 'This old horse knows the track better than me or you and he can win this race. You jump him out, go to the lead and stay there. If you don't win I'll make sure you never ride again – I'll disqualify you for life.'

Back in the betting ring, the price on the favourite grew shorter and some bookies refused to take more bets on him; some of them would be broke if the favourite won. As the big field got ready behind the single strand barrier, the young kid was worried, for he had drawn the rail. He had only ridden a couple of winners and loved the thought of becoming a top jockey. As the barrier stand flew up and the field thundered down the straight for the first time, he gave the old horse a couple of sharp cracks with the whip, and went out to lead by three lengths. Then, as he went out of the straight, he led by six lengths.

The wily old trainer, scratching his head and cursing, made up his mind to sack the young jockey as soon as he returned to the saddling paddock. Yet still he thought the old horse would fail in the last few hundred yards. But as the field turned into the straight he started to curse louder, for the old horse kicked about ten lengths in front. It was the winner in a boil-over. The trainer, now red-faced, flustered and fuming, hurried to the saddling paddock. As the horses returned to the scales the swabbing official, who had backed the old horse at 33-1, called congratulations to the young jockey, then tried to shake hands with the trainer. But his hand was brushed aside as the fuming trainer headed for the young jockey, who had just had his biggest ever win. Before he could dismount, the trainer sacked him in no uncertain terms. Never again would he ride for his stable, he was told. Later that night, when the wily old trainer heard the full story of how the official had won heaps on the old horse, collected his winnings, then headed straight for the city with that day's swabs safely stashed in his car, he had two fights in the pub as a result of being asked how he had gone at the races. At closing time he was helped home, still cursing the bloody young jockey who couldn't ride to orders, and sneaky race officials who could not be trusted with swabs and took it upon themselves to instruct young jockeys.

Mulga laughed as he recalled this episode – he was still not sure if he'd been paid his two bob that week by his employer. Now, as they made plans for Comet's future, they were reminded of the uncertainty of racing: even the best laid plans could go amiss.

Over the next few months as they lay in their swags in the mustering camps, they listened to each other's tales, hopes and dreams. In the clear cold wintry nights they looked up at the stars as they glittered like a million chandeliers. Horse bells tinkled and the hobble chains clinked close by. Mating dingoes howled and from afar came answering calls. The dingoes would hunt in a pack, love and fight until the rising of the sun, then burrow down in hollow logs or caves to sleep until the next sundown.

Sandy had already told Mulga and Bindi of his plan to build a three bedroom house with a big verandah, as well as a septic system toilet and lighting plant. Already a builder had been out to Red Hills and pegged the site of the house and the shed for the lighting plant. Sandy reckoned by the end of the year they would be living in a new house. At last, he said, he would have a big office at one end of the verandah. It was years now since they had taken the first big mob of unbranded cattle from Mulga

Downs, and with rising cattle prices Sandy had already reaped rich rewards from that first illegal muster.

Bindi had told Mulga how Sandy now had to go to Mulga Downs every mail day, and even made other trips to use the phone and order things they hadn't ever worried about before. As Bindi said, Sandy had a beaten track to Mulga Downs these days, and Bindi didn't think it really had anything to do with collecting mail or ordering rations for the last few months. A new housemaid had been employed to serve old Sugar-Bag and his jackaroos as they sat around the table at night in their white starched shirts and ironed trousers and polished boots. She had come from the city, and Sandy had met her in town soon after she arrived. According to Bindi she was taller than Sandy, with black hair, green eyes; a happy friendly sort of girl. She was called Mary. Putting together Sandy's frequent visits to Mulga Downs and the house-building plans, Bindi and Mulga sensed romance was in the air. When Sandy returned from one of his trips to Mulga Downs, Bindi and Mulga would ask him — how were things? Did he have a cup of tea in the kitchen? Did he see Mary? Sandy usually just smiled and said nothing.

Well, they thought, at least next year they would have proper showers, running water, electric lights and toilets.

In fact, Sandy really was in love with Mary, happy if he could talk to her for a few minutes as she hurried around helping in the kitchen and going about her other duties at the big house. He had already asked her, months ahead, to accompany him to the claypan dance held at the Mulga Cup. Even before the droving began he had decided he would be there, whether he had cattle on the road or not. If he was droving at the time he would leave Bindi with the cattle and return for the races. He told himself it was mainly because of Comet.

By now there were only a few months left before the races on Mulga Downs. The three men had decided to give Comet his chance. In a few days they would head north with the horses to move a mob of cattle to the trucking yards at Muddy Gully, a five weeks' trip. Mulga would be horse tailer, looking after all the horses; this would enable him to train Comet while Sandy and Bindi drove the cattle herd to town. Two of Bindi's countrymen were engaged from Black Rock. A few mornings later, Mulga and a young fella called Quart-Pot, a cousin of Bindi's, packed the horses and headed off across bush country to a station about eighty miles away as the crow flies but some two hundred miles by road. It would take them three days to reach the station, where they would join up with the cattle muster. Mulga rode Comet – it was the first time the horse had left Red Hills since he arrived there as a foal.

They set out with over thirty horses altogether. During the daytime the tongues of the horse bells were tied. Hobbles hung from the horses' greenhide neckstraps. Chains rattled and clinked as the horses jogged and trotted, some reluctant to leave their mates back in the yard. But they soon settled down. At the boundary fence they changed horses, leading Comet now as they drove the herd ahead. They thought he might give trouble and gallop back to the mob of mares he ran with. That night, a fair distance from Red Hills, they made camp near a windmill. With a fence behind them, they hobbled the horses, and let loose the tongues of the horse bells. After watering Comet and leading him to a patch of grass amid the feeding horses, they hobbled and sidelined him for the night. The other horses, hobbled with two front feet together, could move freely around, even gallop flat out if they wished. But Comet was hobbled and had another chain from the front feet to one hind leg, which stopped him from moving freely. He was being broken into camp like all the other old horses. Mulga woke before daylight next morning, to the sound of the horse bells nearby. He lit the fire then woke his mate and they ate breakfast. The first streaks of dawn appeared in the east as they rolled their swags, packed the bags, gathered their bridles and walked over to the horses, dark shapes in the soft dawn light. They caught their riding horses and unhobbled the herd; then, mounting bareback, they drove the horses back to the camp. Mulga, deciding that Comet needed more work, rode him again.

The plan was that when they reached the station with the horses, they would take delivery of the cattle at an old bronco yard miles from the station homestead. When they arrived, however, the bronco yard and mustering camp were silent; the station must still be mustering the cattle and they would turn up tomorrow. Next morning, after gathering the horses, Mulga and Quart-Pot sat around in their camp and waited. Soon they saw a tractor coming towards them, towing a trailer. The camp cook had arrived, a wiry old whiskered fellow who greeted them warmly. He was well known to them and they gave him a hand to unpack. Soon he had the billy boiled and told them the cattle would be here this evening – the men were still mustering along the creeks and flats.

This old cook was known in the outback as Ten-Eighty because of the poisonous meals he served up. (Later, Mulga was to learn how he got this nickname.) Mulga often drank with him in town and got on all right with him. He remembered words of wisdom he'd been given when he first started work: 'Never fall out with cooks, they're the ones who feed you. Bosses are nothing, they just give the orders and can only sack you – but the cook, he has to feed you all the time. Always keep in good with cooks, then you can get a cup of tea or a piece of cake at any time of day or night.' Mulga had soon found out this was one of the best pieces of information he had ever received.

Finally Sandy, Bindi and the rest of the crew arrived. They made camp a hundred yards from the station camp. When the musterers appeared with the cattle and drew near the yards, Sandy, Bindi and Quart-Pot caught horses and rode out to help.

The head stockman greeted them – a wizened old bloke, thin and wiry with skin like cracked leather, a whip over his arm and a cigarette that appeared glued to the corner of his mouth. He was called Green-Hide because he resembled a piece of shrivelled up cow hide. He told them that they would have to muster again tomorrow and get more cattle to make up the numbers. He and Sandy decided to kill a bullock that night and take half each. Green-Hide rode into the mob of cattle, selected a killer and shot him. The cattle were then driven away as the men set to skinning and boning the meat on the ground. Back at the camp they salted and halved the meat.

Just before dark all the men from both camps helped to yard the cattle into the big bronco yard. Afterwards they sat around the fires and ate the fresh juicy rib bones cooked on the coals. Sandy and Green-Hide had decided that Sandy and his men would hold the cattle while Green-Hide and his team mustered more; they were sure there were still plenty of cattle down the creek. They should be back by dinner time next day. Then, after they had drafted the herd out on the flat, Sandy could be off next day with his mob bound for Muddy Gully.

They began talking of the town as stockmen always seemed to do out bush – and the chief topic always seemed to be barmaids and waitresses that they had courted and almost won. No mention of outlaw horses they had ridden tonight, only women and the good times. The horse bells rang and tinkled from everywhere, but not a sound came from the yarded cattle. Soon the men were also silent as they retired to their luxury suites: a swag rolled out upon the ground amid Bogan fleas and bindi-eyes as the stars glittered and glowed overhead and shed a soft dim light over the camps.

Next day, as the morning star rose, Mulga and the cook stoked the fire and had a cup of tea. Then in the gloom Mulga headed to where he last heard the horse bells, the grassy flat where they had been hobbled. As he drew near one horse shook itself: that bell was like a guiding light – soon he could make out the dark shapes of horses, some sleeping, some starting to feed. He dismounted, let the night horse go, then caught and saddled Comet, still sidelined. He walked among the herd undoing straps from the horses' legs, then buckling them to the neck straps. He counted his mob, then headed back to the camp. By now the first streaks of daylight began to redden the eastern sky. The men, eating breakfast, stood around the fire. As Mulga walked to the fire he heard the musterers' cook in the other camp shouting loudly, trying to stir the sleeping men: 'Get up, ya lazy bastards, the sun will be up in a moment, you'll be sunburnt in your swags, ya lazy so and so's!'

Over at the drovers' camp the men sat around the fire waiting for the sun to rise to take the cattle from the yard. At last the station men finished eating, saddled up and headed off, while Sandy and his men let the cattle out of the yard to feed. Once the mob was settled Mulga returned, checked the horses and gathered wood for the cook.

By lunchtime the musterers had returned with more cattle. Green-Hide was sure now he had plenty of cattle to make up the droving mob. They all had dinner, then, after changing horses they started up the mob. Holding them out on the flat, they began to draft the unwanted ones from the mob. Soon cattle and men on horseback were racing everywhere, cutting some out, turning some back, the dust started to rise, the horses sweating. One jackaroo, wearing a huge pair of gooseneck spurs and mounted on an old station horse, drove the spurs into him as a bullock raced past. The old horse turned; feeling the cold steel digging into his ribs, he gave one mighty buck, turned in midair and the roo went straight ahead as the old horse went the other way, landing on his head. He lay winded amid the yahoos and cheers from the men, pulling Bogan fleas and bindi-eyes from his face and head and hair. Only his pride was injured. He unbuckled his spurs and put them in his saddle bag, then took the reins of the old horse who stood close by. As Green-Hide told that jackaroo, falling on your head was one good way of saving the soles of riding boots.

Another horse fell as it crashed over a cow on broken ground. Horse and rider went down in a cloud of dust, but the rider was on his feet instantly, gathering the reins as the horse regained his feet. The men and cattle stirred up the dust till at last the mob was drafted and counted. Sandy, now in charge, watered them, then let them feed around. Just before sunset back into the yards they went, for the last undisturbed night's sleep for the drovers.

Next morning the drovers took the mob from the yard and headed off, while the rest of the musterers went out to gather and brand more cattle.

5

Once through the boundary fence, it would take Sandy and Bindi and his mate Quart-Pot, who tended the cattle, about five weeks to reach town. Mulga's job was to look after the horses, help the cook gather wood and water each day, and train Comet to win the Mulga Cup. For the next month or more they would be on their own with over six hundred head of fat bullocks headed for the trucking yards.

The first night they made camp about ten miles away. From now on the cattle would be put on camp at sundown, while all night the men took turns riding around the herd. At daylight off they would move to another camp. The distances they made varied by how far it was to water or grass, sometimes eight, sometimes fifteen miles each day, watering and feeding the cattle, always heading for the railway line and the far off trucking yards. The work was not hard but the men worked long hours from daylight till sunset as well as two or three hours on nightwatch. Each day brought its own experiences, chasing cattle away, meeting other drovers heading out, a lone grader driver repairing the road. Then they would stop and yarn, as the cattle fed around. Once a week, if they happened to be near the dirt track called a highway, the driver of the weekly mail truck, an old-time drover, would always pull up and yarn leaving some week-old newspapers and relaying all the latest scandal from the town. Whenever they killed they always saved some meat for the mailman to take home on his return trip.

Their cook, old Cornbeef Jimmy, did no night watch; each night after the cattle were put on camp he did the dogwatch. While the men had supper he was on watch until seven o'clock. Mulga, as horse tailer, always took first night watch, because he had to rise hours before the other men to gather the horses and have them back on camp before they left their swags. Then he would help the cook to pack, carting water up the steep banks of creeks, filling water drums. After the cook made breakfast he woke the men, then once again rode dogwatch while they ate. Then they saddled their horses, and in the reddening light of dawn moved off to the next camp.

Sometimes there was a cattle rush, but mostly if cattle were fed and watered well they would not rush. Mulga, Bindi and Sandy often talked of cattle rushes and they agreed that cattle that always seemed to rush were not handled properly. Half-starved, thirsty, driven into the ground, these cattle were the ones likely to rush at night. They knew there were drovers and drivers in the game: some men drove their mob, others would simply drive them. When they reached the saleyards or trucking yards you could always see the difference between the mob brought in by the drover and the mob brought in by the driver.

By now Comet had settled down. Each day he would be given exercise. Sometimes he was behind horses, at other times Mulga would give him a fast gallop in the evening as he herded the horses together. At night he was given a feed of grain, then hobbled out with the other horses.

One day a station owner came past with a message from the stock and station agents: the trucking date for the mob of cattle was two weeks away. This gave them plenty of time, but now Sandy had a deadline he could plan the stages of the last few weeks of the trip in detail.

This had been a slow easy trip. The hours were long but not hard with grass and water everywhere. In drought, of course, it was a different story. Then droving became hell. No grass or water, starving cattle, poor horses. It was usually a feast or famine outback, and the seasons decreed whether a droving trip would be hard or easy.

~

Twenty miles from town they passed through a small sheep and cattle station owned by a bloke called Tom. He always let drovers have the use of a paddock for spelling horses, never charging them agistment fees. As Sandy camped on Tom's country, he sent the cook to the station homestead to tell him they were killing a bullock tonight and Tom could take what meat he wanted. This was their way of paying him for the use of the paddock. Late that evening Tom drove up. Mulga had his knives sharpened and they went back to the feeding mob, where Sandy shot a killer from horseback. The men then drove the herd away, leaving Sandy, Tom and Mulga to skin and bone the carcass.

While they worked they talked of the races coming up at Mulga Downs. Tom, a keen racing man, remarked how well Comet looked, and when they told him of their plan to enter him in the Mulga Cup, Tom said he was looking for a stockman to help with mustering for shearing. He had a graded track on the station where he had once worked horses of his own. Now it was overgrown with grass and weeds. But if Mulga would work for him for a month or two, he would grade the overgrown racetrack and Comet could be worked there. His stables had been empty for some years, he told them. This suggestion was well received. It would be ideal for the training of Comet, he would not have to be driven hundreds of miles and become leg weary before the races. Tom had a horse float and when the races were on he would take Comet to Mulga Downs.

By the time they finished boning the carcass, they had agreed that after the delivery of the cattle, Mulga would work for Tom and train Comet on the station. Sandy would go back for another mob of cattle after they finished. Tom produced a bottle of rum and they drank from an old tin mug. Soon they headed back, Sandy to the cattle, Mulga to the horses, Tom to feast at home on the fresh beef. With the trip almost over, the men could see the lights of town at night time, reflected in the sky.

On the last day they finished trucking before the town stirred, then sat around waiting for the pubs and shops to open. After weeks of work, day and night, it gave them satisfaction to have completed a job well done. Now the trip was over they could relax and joke around the fire as Sandy made up and signed their cheques.

Tomorrow Bindi would start out again on his own with the packhorses. After a few days and nights in town, mostly on the booze, the others would head off for another mob of cattle. Mulga and Comet would stop at Tom's place, as it always seemed to be called – no-one referred to it by its real name. If you asked the locals the way to Saltbush Station, they would never be able to tell you, but just mention old Tom's place and they all knew the way. So Comet and Mulga settled down on Saltbush to muster sheep for shearing and to prepare for the Mulga Cup. Mulga cleaned out a stall for Comet, and graded the overgrown racetrack with an old Ferguson tractor, dragging a huge heap of wire netting, which pulled the grass from the ground.

Some mornings Mulga would work Comet on Tom's graded track. Other times Comet would be taken mustering, and in the evening he would be exercised by getting the sheep from the small holding paddocks.

Once shearing started, Tom and Mulga were kept busy mustering and drafting sheep. Mulga slept in the shearer's quarters and at night they all sat and yarned. Mulga soon realised that shearers were a lot like drovers; at night around the shed they talked of booze, women and the town, and cursed the bloody big rough wethers. Only yesterday one shearer struggling with a huge wether had complained to old Tom as he walked past: 'If you're going to breed bloody big rough sheep like these bastards then you'd better start breeding your own bloody sons to shear them. Because I won't be coming back next year.' Old Tom had just grinned and walked on.

To Mulga, the shearers only seemed happy when they were complaining of the sheep, or the climate or the cook. Their conditions were heaven: eight hours a day, no weekend work, a bed and mattress, a roof over their heads at night, living on the best of tucker, big wages. The greasy little rouseabouts earned more than the drovers and if it rained they never got wet. Two smokos a day, sponge cakes and all the rest. But Mulga knew how hard they worked for their money. He listened at night to legends of the shearing sheds, and decided drovers and shearers were both a hard working lot. Many spent their big cheques in outback pubs, on sprees that lasted for weeks on end.

He heard the tale of one bloke, a shearing contractor, who once headed out to a shearing shed where at the last moment the cook pulled out. He set off deciding he would have to cook himself, as they were starting work the next day. Reaching a little one-horse pub on the way to the shed, the shearers in the back of the truck demanded he pull up so they could load up with grog. As the men went inside, the contractor spied a stranger crashed against the wall. Talking to the publican, he learned that a mob of cattle was being trucked tomorrow afternoon; that was why a train with a long line of cattle wagons stood at the siding. The publican told the contractor that no-one around the place was looking for work. By now, the shearers, all pissed and loaded up with cartons of beer and bottles of rum, began crawling into the back of the truck.

The contractor looked once more at the bloke sleeping off the booze against the wall, and as the last few drunken shearers were about to get on the truck, he told them: 'Listen, you bastards, we don't have a cook so you can fight between yourselves who's going to cook tomorrow or you can shanghai that bloke over there.' Immediately two drunken shearers grabbed the arms and legs of the sleeper and tossed him with one mighty heave into the back of the truck. He didn't stir as he landed among the grog, rations and drunken shearers. The old contractor, smiling now, took off in a cloud of dust and they headed out sixty miles. When they reached the shearing shed the contractor helped carry the new cook, still choked, to one of the rooms. Next morning the contractor went to wake his new cook, shaking him roughly and yelling: 'Get up, ya bastard, you have to cook breakfast for twenty men!' At last awake, the stranger wanted to know what was happening – where was he? When told he was at a station and he had been employed last night as a shearer's cook, he began to curse, calling the contractor all the bastards in the world and swearing he was kidnapped. The contractor swore the man had accepted the job in the pub last night and got on the truck himself. Then the newly appointed cook told him: 'Ya silly old bastard, I'm the bloody engine driver from the train that's waiting to load cattle this evening!' Somehow they managed to pacify the engine driver, and while the shearers, seedy from the grog, prepared to start work, the boss drove him back to the railway siding and his train.

One old shearer vouched that the story was true. 'I know that old bastard,' he said. 'He would have taken the train as well as the driver if he could have gotten something out of it.' Mulga enjoyed most of the tales of shearers' cooks, how some would drink all the lemon and vanilla essence, sometimes metho as well, then take off with the ding-bats miles out in the bush.

Shearing meant good money, much better than droving, but Mulga thought these men earned their money the hard way, always governed by the clock and bell, always with a boss looking on. Unlike the droving or station life, where men worked for weeks completely regardless of time. The job had to be done and they did it. And when they'd finished they sat around whether the boss was there or not. They worked to suit the conditions, rising early in summer then resting in the heat of the day. When the day grew cooler they would start work again in the late evening.

Shearing meant a different lifestyle: hurried meals, the shearers cursing the cook and the rouseabout cursing the money-hungry shearer as he watched the clock and caught another sheep just seconds before the boss rang the knock-off bell. In this world of daggy sheep and piles of wool, Mulga realised that the best shearers were paid their true worth, while the learners received only the amount they could earn. In the mustering camps and out droving, on the other hand, all men were paid the same – the stockman with forty years' experience got exactly the same as jackaroos with just four days on the job, who couldn't even saddle a horse. It was the same old argument: for years the cockies and the big company station managers had maintained that being a good stockman was not a trade. Mulga supposed this was simply because the cockies and managers knew little of handling stock themselves, and if they paid everyone the same wages, the workforce would never go on strike as a whole, since the unskilled men outnumbered the skilled. But in the end, Mulga was convinced, this situation must lead to the decline of the pastoral industry as he knew it.

As the shearing continued at Saltbush the weather grew colder. Mulga would rise in the reddish glow of a cold crisp new day and work Comet around the training track. As Comet became fitter, the more eagerly he trotted, cantered or galloped. Everything was in Mulga's hands: he knew he had a good horse and it was up to him whether he became a winner.

If Mulga went off mustering for the day, he would mix feed for Comet and around midday someone else would water and feed him. In the afternoons, if Mulga had time, he would groom Comet and clean out the stall, and as the weather became colder late at night he would walk to the stable before retiring to get out another horse rug. To Mulga, training a racehorse was a bit like droving cattle – a twenty-four hours a day job in rain, hail or shine. The horse had to be fed and watered even if it was not worked. One horse was no easier to train than twenty; you still had to be on deck those twenty-four hours.

Yet Mulga found pleasure in those hours spent with Comet before dawn and after sunset. He was not paid to train the horse, he did it for the love of doing something properly and hoping to see the result on the racetrack. That would be his reward – to see Comet win. Although it was Mulga who had found Comet years before, an orphaned foal, as soon as he'd taken him back to Red Hills Sandy had begun to refer to him as 'their' horse. Mulga realised that Comet belonged to Red Hills Station. Bindi benefitted by breeding some of his mares to Comet: both Sandy and Bindi would reap the rewards of Comet's foals. Mulga, always on the move, had no use for horses of his own. It would be enough for Mulga if Comet won, pitting his skills against the other racehorses. Mulga's reward would be his sense of achievement.

Now the shearing was about to finish on Saltbush. The shearers packed away their combs and cutters, the rousies swept and hosed the floor. The woolpresser worked the lever and the last of the wool was pressed into bales then weighed and marked with the Saltbush brand, to be taken away, sold and sent to some foreign land. The shearers waited around the shed as the last sheep was shorn, the wages tallied up and cheques made out. Soon the shed would be deserted, the men scattered – some to another shed, some to live it up in town until their cheques were spent. Peace and quiet returned to Saltbush Station.

As the Mulga Cup drew nearer and Comet became fitter, Mulga would go to town some weekends. He would drink and listen to the yarns of an old retired drover called Dasher – no-one seemed to know his real name or where he was born. Dasher claimed he had been on every stock route in Australia, and would talk of his experiences for hours. One night he told Mulga his favourite tales that he claimed was true: the real story of the Min-min light, which every bushman claimed to have seen, that mystery light that bobbed and weaved, glimmered and glowed, changing colour, appearing then vanishing as it danced just above the ground, seeming to come closer then fading into the distance. Mulga himself had seen lights at night in outback camps, but had always sought some simple explanation – a car's headlights, perhaps. But then he would realise there were no roads.

Once, in timbered country, he had watched a glittering light appear low in the western sky, appearing to dance and weave as it changed colours from red to green or bluish white, a throbbing pulsating glow. Even after watching it for five minutes he could not be sure whether the light moved behind the trees or not. Then it would be gone, leaving Mulga to wonder whether it was the evening star playing games or the real Min-min light.

Now Mulga and Dasher settled down in a corner of the bar. Taking a pocket-knife and tobacco plug from his pocket, Dasher filled his pipe and lit up. At last Mulga was going to hear the real story of the Min-min light: for Dasher declared the light was no mystery at all to him. Years ago, he and his mate, the cook known as Ten-Eighty, were employed by a drover who started off with the biggest mob of cattle in the world. They started out from the biggest station in the world – it was so far west you had to go past sundown to get there. They were a wild mob of cattle; at the beginning of the trip they rushed every night. However, they were soon tamed by the best stockmen in the world. Dasher, of course, was one of these; he claimed that was how he earned his name – when the cattle rushed at night he was always the first to dash to the lead and swing them around. And it was on this same trip, he said, that 'Ten-Eighty' got his name. For his mate Barry, as he was then called, was given the job of cooking for the trip. And before Dasher embarked on his story of the Min-min light, he first related the tale of how Barry became 'Ten-Eighty'.

After a few weeks on the road, the men complained about Barry's cooking. They fell sick with severe stomach pains and claimed they were being poisoned by the tucker they were forced to eat. At last one night, as the men sat down for supper, they looked into the bedourie oven and refused to eat the mixture they saw, demanding the Boss should sack the cook and hire a new one. Then Barry said: 'All right, you bastards, if you don't want my bloody tucker I'll throw it out. The bloody dingoes can eat it.' So he carried it about fifty yards away and tipped it out. After a scratch meal of corn beef and soggy damper, the men settled down for the night, reassured by the Boss that another cook would be found.

That night, for some reason, the dingoes seemed to be more numerous, and their howls were pitiful. Next morning, the men saddled their horses, stirred the sleeping cattle and set out from the camp. As they passed the remains of Barry's cooking, they saw four dead dingoes around the mixture and another three dogs wobbling and staggering as they tried to escape, while six more dingoes sat and howled on a ridge a few hundred yards away. Dasher, as he described these events to Mulga, claimed no-one had ever heard such a mournful sound in their life. The horse tailer, meanwhile, reached for the gun, for dog scalps were worth two quid apiece in those days. But as he took aim, the Boss yelled out: 'Don't shoot! If those poor bastards could eat Barry's tucker and survive, they deserve their freedom!' As the herd headed east and the dingoes on the ridge howled louder, Barry was christened 'Ten-Eighty' after 10-80, the most potent poison ever used to control the dingo. Mulga himself knew this name had stuck to the unfortunate cook, but whether Dasher's story was true, he just did not know.

He also recalled that one time when he was drinking in town with Ten-Eighty, the old cook had told him how Dasher himself had earned his nickname – not for dashing to the lead of stampeding cattle in the night, the cook maintained, but because he was always the first to dash to the safety of the nearest tree when the cattle rushed. Mulga thought of this now, as he waited for Dasher to tell the story of the Min-min light. Meanwhile, he ordered rums and beer chasers. Dasher knocked the ashes from his pipe, refilled it, swallowed the rum in one swig, sipped the beer, then continued his story.

He told of months on the road, dust storms, dry stages, flooded rivers. They kept going east and reached the land of the small cockie stations, with fences everywhere and gates to open all the time. At last, after the biggest and longest cattle droving trip in the world, the cattle were delivered. After delivery of the cattle the horses were turned loose for a few weeks' spell before the long trip home. Dasher and Ten-Eighty had agreed to take the horses back home. Their pockets full of money, they booked into a hotel for a well-earned rest. With the horses safe in a paddock, they settled down for a good old-fashioned spree and for the next few weeks they downed the rum. (At this point Dasher started to talk of the barmaid he almost won, and Mulga wondered if he would ever get to the Min-min light.) He ordered another rum for Dasher, who told of how he wined and dined the barmaid, then discovered she was married with four kids – after her husband had punched him in the mouth and told him to keep away.

At last, after weeks on the rum, their money was getting low so Dasher and Ten-Eighty decided to muster the horses and head back out west. Loading the pack bags with some tucker and more bottles of rum, they set off. Neither were in the best of health, both almost pickled with alcohol. Their heads seemed to split with each step the horses took. Each night as they got farther away from the town they downed the rum from the pack bags.

Weeks later they passed through a little town where they again filled the pack bags, mostly with rum. By now they had started to argue about things at night as they sat and drank. Then one night, miles from anywhere as they sat around the fire they realised that for the first time in over a month they had no rum. Drinking black tea, which they had to imagine was rum, they stared into the fire. Then Dasher looked up and saw a car light coming across the rolling plain ahead. 'Someone's coming!' he told Ten-Eighty. 'He might have a drink.' A little later they looked up and saw the light still in the same place. 'He must have broken down,' Dasher said, but Ten-Eighty argued that the bloody light was moving and changing all the time. Even as they looked the light appeared to move, to glitter brightly then fade. Then it began to bob and weave, changing colours. Both men now believed it was the Min-min light they saw. 'I wonder what makes it glow and dance?' Ten-Eighty said to Dasher. 'It's just over there – why don't we take the night horses and catch the bloody thing? Solve the riddle of the Min-min light once and for all!' So both men, almost in the ding-bats after ages on strong black rum, caught the best night horses in the herd and saddled up.

Ten-Eighty grabbed a rope and fashioned it into a loop, tying one end around his now bulging stomach. Out on the plain the light seemed only yards away. 'Come on, let's get the bastard!' Ten-Eighty yelled as he swung the rope and let the night horse have his head. Dasher's eyes seemed to light up as he told of the night chase. For about an hour they galloped and weaved across the plain. The light would be just ahead – then as they urged the horses faster, it would disappear, only to reappear behind them. It faded then grew brighter, shedding its ghostly glow as it bobbed and weaved across the plain. By now the horses were in a lather of sweat and foam. Raving about the tricky bloody light, Ten-Eighty raced on once more as it appeared ahead. With one last effort he threw the rope, in a desperate bid to capture the elusive Min-min light, the riddle that had mystified men for ages. As he tossed the loop he was amazed to feel a tug on the end of the rope. The slack raced through his hands as the horse came to a halt. The rope tightened around his waist: with one mighty tug he was pulled from the saddle. As he hit the ground head-first and was dragged along on his stomach, still clutching the rope, he raised his head above the black dirt, burrs and dry grass, calling: 'I've got the bloody bastard! I've got him!' By this time the thing on end of the rope was still. Dasher dismounted and came forward. Ten-Eighty began to pull the rope and the Min-min light towards him as he lay on the ground. Then for a moment the light went out.

Dasher reached forward in the dark and felt something soft. Becoming bolder, he felt a long neck and legs, then a lot of feathers. 'I think we've caught and killed a bloody emu, mate!' he yelled to Ten-Eighty, who was still spitting dirt and grass from his mouth as he struggled to his feet.

The mysterious light still glowed, and Dasher reached down to see what it was. Protruding from the emu's arse was a torch! He pulled it out and shone it around. 'Bloody good torch,' he said, 'I wonder how it got there.' 'Bugger the bloody torch,' Ten-Eighty answered, 'what sort of batteries are inside it? Don't you realise this bloody light has been glowing for over a hundred years? They have to be the best batteries in the world.' Dasher unscrewed the end of the torch. After one hundred years the Min-min light went out. Ten-Eighty, still eager to discover the brand of batteries, struck a match. Lying in the dirt alongside the dead emu were Eveready torch batteries.

At this point Dasher stopped talking and wiped his mouth with his shirt-sleeve as Mulga ordered another rum and beer chaser. Dasher then swore this was the true story of the Min-min; to prove it he had the torch and batteries, which still shone bright when turned on. He also claimed that no more lights were ever seen across that misty hazy plain where the emus roam. Morning mist and haze may still reflect mirages of homestead or windmill, but the Min-min light has never been seen since that night.

Then, as Dasher drank another rum, he told Mulga: 'You can have the torch, mate, in exchange for a bottle of O.P. rum.' And that was how Mulga became the proud possessor of the best torch in the world. After that, when droving stock and watching the herd at night, he would often look across the plains but never see that bobbing, weaving light that used to come and go. Only occasional car headlamps, camp fires glowing afar off, and the evening star, which seemed to pulsate and throb as it changed colours in the wintry evening sky. And Mulga realised that of late no-one seemed to speak of the Min-min ... So maybe Dasher and Ten-Eighty *had* solved the riddle once and for all.

Back at Saltbush Station, Mulga put the finishing touches to Comet's training, and at last the big day arrived when Comet and Mulga headed for Mulga Downs and the races.

All along the dry creek and scattered among the mulga and gydgea trees tents were pitched, and alongside them were tethered the racehorses, grass-fed and corn-fed, some tame, others real yang-yangs who would buck or bolt when the rider mounted, perhaps not even making it to the start. The last glimpse the owner might have of one of these horses was as it bolted through the trees after tossing its rider.

Around the makeshift bar crowded owners, stockmen and labourers. A couple of bookies were calling odds. The women, despite the dust and flies, were decked out in the latest fashions, their once shining white shoes covered in dust as the ground turned to red powder from the tramp of many feet.

Mulga met up with Sandy and Mary and Bindi, and they planned their tactics for the race. Bindi, the lightest of the three men, was talked into riding Comet in the Mulga Cup. They had an exercise saddle loaned by old Tom from Saltbush, but no racing colours, so Bindi dressed in stockman's gear, R.M. Williams riding boots, Levis, and a bright green cowboy shirt, the flashiest one he owned. Then all the jockeys, some in polished boots and shining silks, others, like Bindi, in stockman's gear, headed for the start. As the spectators shouted encouragement to the horses they had backed, the Mulga Cup was off around the graded track. Soon the red cloud of dust that was the field reached the straight, where on the inside of the track some posts and rails had been put up over the last few furlongs, to keep the horses on a straight course for the winning-post. As the field made the slight bend into the straight and the leading horses became recognisable, Mulga, Sandy and Mary gave a loud cheer. A couple of horses racing outside Comet could not make the turn: they went bush straight into the trees. Now Comet was alone, six lengths ahead of the field, most of which was still hidden by the huge red dust cloud. He had won!

After the victory, the others celebrated, while Mulga led Comet away from the crowd, to a yard of rails tied to some trees. A short distance away he recognised an old drover called Jam-Tin, who had a horse set to run in the next race. He was getting his horse ready, helped by the 'Preacher', who was as well known for the rum he drank as for the sermons he delivered when visiting outback towns and isolated stations. Mulga saw that both the Preacher and Jam-Tin had had a few drinks and were half-pissed. A bottle of rum stood against the butt of a tree. As Mulga watched, he overheard Jam-Tin tell the Preacher he was putting a hundred quid on his horse. He wanted the Preacher to place the bet, as he would be given better odds than himself – and to make sure his horse won he told the Preacher he would have to say a prayer for the underfed, scraggly looking creature, whose back and sides were covered in dried mud. Mulga guessed that the wily Jam-Tin had let it roll in a patch of mud to make its appearance rougher and maybe increase the odds offered by the tight-wad bookmakers.

Then, as Mulga attended to Comet under the shady trees, he saw the Preacher kneel down in the red dust, with Jam-Tin beside him. Their eyes closed tightly, they prayed for the victory of the mud-covered horse with its knotted mane and tail. After they had finished the call came for starters in the next race. Both men helped themselves to another nip of rum apiece and the Preacher walked away to place the bet. Jam-Tin saddled up – then, just as he was about to lead the horse away, he took from his pocket a tobacco tin. Mulga thought this was strange; he knew Jam-Tin never smoked. As he watched, Jam-Tin opened the tin, wet one finger in his mouth, dipped it into the tin, then wiped it on his horse's tongue. The animal must have a sore tongue, Mulga thought to himself as he headed back to the crowd to watch the race. As the horses made their way to the start, many joked about the appearance of the drover's scraggy old horse. Then, as the horses reached the starting line, that scraggy old horse began to dance and prance. Maybe he didn't have a sore tongue after all, Mulga thought … maybe Jam-Tin had given his horse something else.

The field jumped away; once more a huge red dust cloud blanketed most of it. But ten lengths ahead of that dust cloud was the old drover's horse, and that was how they finished: the drover's horse first, the thick rest dust cloud second. Mulga spied Jam-Tin and the Preacher elated by their success, then as he watched, he heard a young stockman cursing loudly that he had lost his bet, and saw the Preacher place one hand on the shoulder of the cursing man. 'You should not use the Lord's name in vain, my boy,' said the Preacher. 'You will never hear me swearing.'

That night there was merry-making by the light of a camp fire. Sandy, Mary, Mulga, Bindi, the Preacher, Jam-Tin and many others danced and sang the night away. And Sandy and Mary asked the Preacher to marry them as soon as the new house was finished at Red Hills. At Mulga Downs that day, Comet won the first of many victories he would have in the Mulga Cup over the years. He was destined to become a famous racehorse and the sire of great stock horses in the future.

6

The years passed swiftly. Bindi and Mulga continued to work for Sandy from time to time. Sandy and Mary, now married, had a son. Bindi divided his time between Red Hills, Black Rock and droving. Red Hills was now stocked with quality cattle. Sandy had already begun to buy and sell cattle; the foundation of his wealth was well established. Mulga came and went, sometimes in the city, sometimes in the bush, working for Sandy, taking mobs of cattle on the stock routes and driving them to the markets. It was after one such droving trip that Sandy returned to Red Hills and discovered that Comet was missing.

He had returned to Red Hills after months of droving. At first he was not worried about Comet, thinking he must be somewhere around the big bush paddock with a few mares. He drove around the waters checking out the stock. Around the boundary fence, he saw where a mob of horses had been driven along. The tracks were weeks, maybe months old. They could have been the mustering horses on Black Rock, moving from camp to camp.

As Sandy drove around, he saw most of his horses; he knew the little mobs that ran together. Like humans, horses stuck together; some, inseparable, would go berserk if they were taken away from their mates. After a few days there was still no sign of Comet. One morning he saddled up to see if he could find him. Perhaps he had been crippled and was too lame to move around. Looking for tracks, he saw where the horses came and went from the water. A lot of the tracks he could easily recognise by their sizes and the numbers in the herd. He knew where certain mobs always grazed. He looked at the old heap of horse manure piled up where stallions always left their calling card. They would always sniff out the piles where they had been before and leave their manure on top of the previous pile. Bushmen could always tell if stallions were around just by looking at the pile. Now, as Sandy rode around, he began to worry in earnest. Everywhere he rode he saw the heaps of old manure left by Comet, but no fresh manure on any of the piles. He began to think maybe he was dead, bitten by a snake, or else kicked by one of the mares, his leg broken, perishing in the paddock. For three days Sandy rode about. He realised, judging by the heaps of manure, that Comet had not been around for a long time. He must be dead. All the other horses seemed to be accounted for, but it seemed that the pride and joy of Red Hills was dead. With a heavy heart Sandy gave up the search.

Mary, who was pregnant again, tried to console him. She knew how much the horse meant, not only to Sandy, but to Mulga and Bindi as well. Of all the horses that roamed on Red Hills he was clearly their favourite. They treated him as a pet. Yet, she told Sandy as they watched some mares and foals come to the windmill to drink, all was not lost. There were plenty of young horses. The foals galloped and wheeled about, bucked and kicked out as they played around the mares. Sandy smiled sadly as he sat on the verandah.

As the hot summer months continued Sandy fenced and repaired the yards and did all the small jobs around the station. Bindi came back from Black Rock and then went walkabout, as the white man would say in his ignorance of such matters. Walkabout to the black man was something more than just going bush. It was like a pilgrimage to the sacred sites, the Dreaming places, just as Christians visit the Holy City of Jerusalem, or Moslems visit Mecca. The missions tried to force the black people to go to church to pray on Sundays to an alien God. But when the black man went walkabout he was paying homage to spiritual beliefs, renewing his affinity with the land. Not a God in the image of man, but the land itself, the most holy. Everything came from the land and everything returned to the land.

Now Bindi and the remnants of his tribe were on their pilgrimage through their ancestral homeland, much of which covered Red Hills Station. The rock hole, cave paintings, ancient symbols etched deep in the hard red rock, the stone arrangement. While they were camped at the rock hole Sandy came by and found them. He spoke to Bindi for a while. Bindi now owned a four-wheel drive, a rifle: no more stone-age weapons. Yet, as Sandy later remarked, this was the only time he had ever seen Bindi really happy and contented. But even Bindi knew that his way of going walkabout was changing. Even now many tribal mobs went walkabout in motor cars. And when Sandy offered to kill a bullock and give them some flour, tea, sugar and salt, Bindi accepted. Being wise in the ways of the white man, he knew the bullock would not be one of Sandy's. It would be one of the neighbour's cattle.

That evening while Bindi and his mob camped at the rock hole, Sandy and Mary came out in the Land Rover. While Mary and the women waited at the rock hole, Sandy, Bindi and the men drove off to kill the bullock. The women built the fire, heaping up the log so that there would be plenty of coals when the meat arrived. As they waited for the men to return, the women busied themselves with mixing up the flour and making johnny-cakes on the ashes. Waiting for the meat, Mary and her son ate the johnny-cakes, talking and laughing with the always smiling black women. Little Sandy played with the other children. Mary, who had not had a great deal of experience with Aborigines, wondered how these people, with apparently nothing in the world, could be so happy and carefree. She did not realise that when they went walkabout they were like Christians in church.

Only their church was the land and nature itself. Their smiles were not forced, their laughter came from the heart. They were truly contented, with an inner glow Mary had seen on the faces of people of her own race when they believed their prayers had been answered.

At last the men returned. In the back of the Land Rover, stacked on bushes was the carcass of the beast, boned and cut up. Then as the sun sank they began to cook the pieces of meat, curly gut and sweet breads. No knives or forks needed here as they feasted on the neighbour's juicy, freshly killed meat and talked of many things well into the night, until at last Sandy and Mary departed, leaving some of the meat for Bindi.

Sandy had told Bindi of Comet's disappearance and how he was most likely dead somewhere in the paddock. Bindi said he would look out for his remains. He also mentioned that the horse tracks on the Black Rock boundary were not made by station horses being driven from camp to camp, but by a drover known as Forklift. He and another bloke owned a small starvation block of land miles to the north. The country was very poor and they scraped to make ends meet. They were not a very popular pair with anyone because of their habit of taking anything that was not welded down – hence the name 'Forklift'. Another bad habit they had was employing men for droving, mainly Murris from the town, and paying them with rubber cheques, which always bounced. In all they were a very unsavoury pair, Forklift and his mate, dirty in fights, dirty in appearance.

They had double-banked and bashed up a lot of men who had complained about their wages, and there were a lot of characters who would have liked to meet them alone out in the bush.

Bindi had told Sandy that the two had taken a short cut back to their station after a droving trip, and Sandy began to wonder if Comet was really dead. Bindi said he might be able to get help from his countrymen farther north. They often went walkabout to the area where Forklift and his mate lived. Before the summer was over he might be able to have one of them check out the horses. There was always the chance they could have taken Comet. Some mares may have been in season as they drove their horses past and Comet could have been enticed into the herd, then caught and ridden away.

With some hope that Comet still lived, Sandy waited for word from Bindi's mates. Comet was well known to many men of the outback as most attended the Mulga Downs races and over the years had seen him win the cup on four occasions. Any stockman who had seen him once would hardly forget the imposing looking rich red bay with a white star on his forehead. To a bushman horses were like humans; even in a herd of hundreds each was different from the others, easily identifiable from the next.

Bindi returned to Black Rock and Sandy worked his station. Christmas came and went. Bindi was on another station for a few weeks' mustering, then headed for Muddy Gully where he met up again with Mulga.

He told Mulga about Comet and how Sandy could not find any trace of him dead or alive. He also told how Forklift and his mate had driven their horses back past Red Hills. Sandy came to town for the weekend, and the three of them met at the hotel. In the bar Sandy told them that Mary had gone to the city to have her baby. Then their talk turned to Comet. It seemed he was still alive on the station of Forklift and his mate. Bindi told them how his countrymen miles to the north had gone on their usual walkabout over their tribal territory. Many of these men worked most of the year on the surrounding stations; many were top horsemen and stockmen. Most couldn't read or count. Their book was the land· the tracks upon it were like the pages. They also seemed to have an uncanny ability of knowing one horse from another, even in the dark while horse tailing for drovers or mustering camps, rising before dawn to bring the horses back to camp, maybe fifty or sixty head. They could always tell if there were a few horses missing, but not by counting. They would just say, 'Old Bay horse and his mate, little pony fella and another mare, one that bucks and bolts sometimes, the one that threw you against the tree last year.' This was how they kept tally of the horses they were in charge of, they knew each one individually.

Some of these men had told Bindi that while they were on walkabout they had seen Comet. He now ran in a dead-end canyon, narrow at the entrance. A few rails across the mouth of the canyon stopped the horses straying. These tribal men, who had no time for Forklift because of the way he treated their people, were sure the stallion that ran there with a few mares was Comet. They had seen him many times at Mulga Downs Picnic Races; he was the type of horse that stood out in the herd, beautifully proportioned.

Now Sandy, Bindi and Mulga talked about how to recapture Comet. Should they notify the police? After much discussion they decided it might not be wise to let the police know anything. If they headed out to investigate, Forklift and his mate, who listened to everything on the Galah session of the Flying Doctor network, would know the police were on their way and might get rid of Comet so as to have no evidence. It would be simple to drive the herd out of the canyon, shoot Comet and take the mares back. Even if Comet's body was found they could easily claim the carcass was that of a brumby stallion. Slash the hide, cut out the brand, cut up the meat, put some strychnine on it and claim they were poisoning dingoes. Then Comet would surely be lost forever.

Both Bindi and Mulga had been through the country in question and knew how isolated it was. They talked of going and bringing Comet back. They could ride there in about three days. After the rains the property was isolated for months by road and there was no air strip on the station. The more they talked of how to get Comet back, the more they became convinced they would have to do the job themselves. At last Mulga and Bindi decided they would return to Red Hills for a few weeks' mustering, break in some horses and get ready for the droving season. They would then decide what action to take. As Sandy headed back to Red Hills, Bindi and Mulga promised they would join him there in a few days' time. They passed the weekend with their old Murri mates, and they learned that Forklift and his mate were holidaying in the city. Their station would look after itself – the few springs and a couple of waterholes in the creek were full. The cattle they ran roamed their block of thousands of acres with only the boundary fence to hold them in. The place ran itself for most of the year when the men were away droving, fencing or mustering.

As Bindi and Mulga headed out after their weekend in town they still talked about Comet. The countryside was lush and green after good summer rains. Birds rose from the ground and filled the sky in great flocks as they drove past on the built-up dirt highway, more corrugated than ever. They passed through mulga scrub and sandy soil, forests of gydgea trees and open black soil plains where emus ran in mobs of thirty or forty. This was the land of plenty. Cattle and sheep fed across the paddocks where the open grassy plain seemed to go on forever. The land of lost horizons. Both Bindi and Mulga remarked on these things, looking across the hazy distance where a windmill appeared to be suspended in the sky. It was a land of contrasts; one moment the open black soil plains, then mulga forest or the eroded ancient red hills. Stunted brush and trees clung to the hills, the tops below the summit a mass of crumbled rock, with shallow caves where kangaroos, wallabies and dingoes watched men in cars and on horseback who always seemed to come and go. Unlike the emus and turkeys they would lie low until evening, then, as the sun sank, venture forth to feed.

Driving out, Bindi and Mulga met an old grader driver they knew trying to repair the road. If the stockman's life was lonely, the grader driver's life was more so. He worked alone, while musterers and drovers always had company in the camps. Out in the remote shires, the grader driver kept the hundreds of miles of dirt roads open and passable. At night, miles from anywhere, he camped where sunset found him. Most did not even have a dog for company. Dogs did not last long as pets, with poisoned baits scattered across the land in their millions. The aerial baiting campaign killed some dingoes, birds and God knows what else. There were always arguments about the worth of baiting. Most bushmen argued that the dingo only ate the weakest animals that would probably die anyway. When mustering for branding the dingo would follow the mobs closely. As the herd was mustered, some weak cows or crippled calves would begin to drop out. It was not practical to hold up the muster of thousands of cattle for one lame or weak animal so they would be left behind, to become a feast for the hunting dingoes.

Dingoes were a greater menace in the sheep country. A lot of them seemed to have bred with tame dogs; they were not the true dingo, which seemed to kill only for food. On the sheep stations the dogs often killed for fun, eating only the sheep's kidney. A dingo bitch could teach her pups to kill hundreds in a night. Mulga had even seen the station sheep dog do the same thing and the dingo get the blame. Another thing the men had noticed was that out in the land of the dingo, in unfenced pastures, there was no sign of feral cats or wild pigs. Kangaroos were few and emus scarce. It was the foreign animals, the sheep and cattle, that were in plague proportions in the land of the dingo. What a price man had paid in his efforts to exterminate the dingo! What did most damage to the land, what of the balance of nature? Bindi, Mulga and Sandy often talked of these things. Often they had seen the land flogged bare, not a blade of grass for miles with sheep, cattle and horses walking skeletons, carcasses littered around an almost dried-up waterhole. The stock bogged down, too weak to move. Even the alien brumby and the dingo himself dead or dying in the mud. Then, as the hot dry wind swept the land the dust clouds rose from the parched and barren landscape. Sometimes it blew for days and when it cleared the dust and topsoil was gone forever across the ocean. Then, as the hard cloven hooves of horses, cattle and sheep trod on the barren land it became more chipped. With each step the imprint of the animal was left upon the ancient soil to help erode it further. When drought took over it blew away. When rain fell once again, the chipped and eroded soil was washed away.

Around the fire at night bushmen talked long into the night on these subjects. Many believed there should be some form of restriction on the number of stock that grazed the land. In the marginal grazing areas only emus, roos and camels, with feet that were adapted to the environment, should be allowed to graze. Of the imported animals, only the camel was suited to the land. The soft feet of the emu and roo had taken thousands of years to evolve to the land; like the soft round feet of the camel, they did not make imprints in the earth as they walked. Why not market the roo, emu, and camel meat and leather? That would most likely help the land, not kill it as it had been killed for over one hundred years. The meat of these animals would be good as if not better than beef or mutton.

'How long?' This was the question they asked among themselves. Unlike the men in the big houses whose only interest was balancing their books to make profits. Forever trying to increase the herd, yet not putting anything back into the land. Building a fence, calling their work 'improvements', putting down tanks then doubling their herds, putting down artesian bores, some turned on for a hundred years. Over a million gallons of water flowed each day from some, most emptying into bore drains. For miles they snaked across the land, but the bulk of the water evaporated in the hot summer sun. In the bush towns the battler who tried to grow a lawn or a vegetable garden would be summonsed for using too much water. Yet those giant taps flowed unchecked. Would they flow for another hundred years, or would they be regulated?

These were just a few of the things they talked of. Mulga sensed that even though people were isolated in the outback, they seemed to have a better understanding of many things, politics, the economy, overseas issues. Bush people always seemed to read the newspapers more, even if they were outdated. In the early morning and at night, everyone listened to the news service on the radio, while city people would watch for hours some bat-and-ball game.

Now Bindi and Mulga pulled up to have a yarn with the grader driver, whose caravan trailer was stacked with a water tank and enough drums of fuel to last for weeks. Always eager to talk was the grader driver, eager for news of the town or some old newspaper. He boiled the billy and over a cup of tea they talked of everything from how bad mosquitoes were to Common Market problems. The brawls, the scandals, who slept with whom, the latest barmaids in the town, who was working where.

A grader driver seemed to know just what every station was doing for over a hundred miles in each direction. Everyone going and coming stopped and asked how he was and if he needed or wanted anything from the stores. Sometimes a bottle of rum was produced and work was forgotten for the rest of the day. But if the grader driver worked five hours today, then he'd often work twelve the next. Sometimes he would talk and drink till the wee hours, then snatch a few hours' sleep. But these men from the bush, whether drinking half the night away or not would always wake as the first red streaks of dawn lightened the eastern sky. They would rise at once, eat and start work. Most never carried watches, they ate when they were hungry, started work when it became light and finished when the work for the day was done, sometimes after only a few hours, sometimes after dark.

After a night on the booze with old Mick, Bindi and Mulga rose at dawn. Mick was already refuelling the grader and checking the oil. Then, with a 'See you later' they parted as the sun rose above the horizon.

When Bindi and Mulga reached Mulga Downs Station they pulled up at the stockmen's quarters, where they were met by the cowboy, a grizzled old bloke whose job it was to look after the milking cows, the wood supply for the station cook and take orders from the bosses' wife, tend her flower garden if she had one, and feed the fowls. The cowboy never left the station yard – unlike the American cowboy, who seemed to gallop everywhere shooting off his gun in the air. One thing for sure, it was an insult to call a drover or stockman a cowboy, as some now seemed to. Most stockmen would never think of themselves as a cowboy. They believed they could learn little or nothing from the American cowboy in the handling of stock, droving or riding bucking horses.

As they talked to the station cowboy this day, he complained about the load of work he had to do and the way old Sugar-Bag treated his men. A lot of the bosses knew when the cowboy and the stockmen needed a break. He'd give them a few days off in town to spend their money, then back they would come for another few months. But old Sugar-Bag had no idea of these things and how to work his men.

Bindi and Mulga learned, in fact, that the cowboy had just pulled out and was waiting for the mail truck. He told them that Sugar-Bag had said that if he left he would never be employed at Mulga Downs again, calling him all the 'shiftless so and so's' under the sun as he handed him his cheque. The cowboy had taken the cheque and listened to Sugar-Bag's bullshit. Then he said: 'I wouldn't like to see any misfortune befall you, you old bastard, but I hope all your fowls turn into emus and kick your fowlhouse down, you overgrown old marsupial!' Soon the mail truck arrived and the cowboy took off already licking his lips and thinking of the pub.

Arrived at Red Hills at last, Bindi and Mulga talked with Sandy about what they would do for the coming year. Mary was now in the city with her mother, awaiting the birth of her second child. Although they were offered spare rooms on the verandah of the house, Bindi and Mulga still preferred to sleep in the big old shed.

That night after supper, they sat on the verandah, and stretched out on the hard boards. After a hot searing day the cool breeze was refreshing. Although it was still hot Sandy wanted his cattle branded before he began droving for the year. Prices were now high for cattle and he wanted to sell some while the market was in short supply. In a few months the big stations would all start mustering and turning off their fat cattle. If he sold now they would bring much higher prices.

They argued about the best way to get Comet back, and at last agreed that Bindi and Mulga should go to get him. They would take a few horses and ride across country. They would cut through the top end of Black Rock where Bindi knew every inch of the country, keeping away from the roads (really only two-wheel tracks). At this time of the year none of the musterers would be working; they were waiting for the land to dry out and the summer heat to cool. They reckoned they would take six days to get to where Comet was held and to return. They had also confirmed that Forklift and his mate were still holidaying in the city.

7

Next morning early they checked their saddles and pack bags. Sandy filled their packs with enough food to last them, and also supplied an old Winchester rifle, and a spare bridle and halter for Comet. He didn't state what the gun was for, just said: 'You'd better take this, you never know who you might run into when you get there.' They cooked a lot of corn beef, adding a few tins of meat and pouring some flour into the canvas bag. They packed enough bread for a few days; after that it would be too hard and dried to eat, then they could make a damper. Back at Red Hills, Sandy would stay and answer the radio; he would have an alibi if anything happened and Forklift went to the police – which they were sure wouldn't happen as he stole the horse in the first place. They had also decided that when they got back with Comet they would not say anything to anyone about it. But if they did run into the men they would kick the shit out of them. Now, with everything ready for the morning, the three men turned in.

★

Even before the glow of dawn lit up the sky, they mustered the horses, and by the time the first ray of sunlight appeared, Bindi and Mulga headed off. Once away from the station the horses settled down. They had been on many droving trips and would not stray at night. They drove seven head of horses before them, using three packhorses. They also had three changes of saddle horses, as the days would be hot and the going hard. The horses would have to be changed two or three times a day.

Through the boundary fence Bindi took the lead. He headed bush, away from the road that ran along the boundary fence. With Bindi in the lead and Mulga on the tail the horses followed Bindi across stony mulga-covered ridges and open soft red soil. Everywhere they noticed cattle and calves unbranded, and it dawned on Mulga that if they were seen or came upon anyone, even here they would have a lot of explaining to do, men and horses on someone else's country. This was the top end of Black Rock. The station house was about fifty miles away to the south-west. They very occasionally came here, only to muster. The only roads were the bush tracks that led from camp to camp as the men mustered the country each year, over mostly unfenced pastures. The station covered over a million acres. Sometimes there was a boundary fence and a few holding paddocks were scattered across the cattle empire. Some parts of the station remained unvisited for years.

As they drove their horses through a grey-green wilderness of mulga and gydgea scrub they felt no sense of isolation, for everywhere they looked they saw life. Birds, lizards, snakes, emus, roos, dingoes and cattle. Sometimes a fleeting glimpse of racing brumby herds. From their tracks they could tell what animals had passed, but there was no sign of human presence.

By midday they came upon a windmill. Here they watered the horses, then kept going for another mile. Among the stony mulga ground they found a gilgai full of water, and here they rested, ate and changed horses, then headed north once more.

The ground and the country began to change. Creeks were mostly dry – they drained the country to the east. That night they camped by a small waterhole, which would be dry in a few weeks. After hobbling the horses, they ate around a small fire, and Bindi told Mulga how he had gone north during the wet, in search of a wife. He told Mulga how the elders had chosen the right wife for him. They said, 'She is the right one for you, she is the right meat, that's the proper one for you.' Before long he would go north again and take her for his tribal wife. Bindi said he could have taken a wife from the women around the town, but had decided to follow tradition by marrying someone described as 'the right meat' for him. This was something now forgotten by most scattered remnants of the tribes. As Bindi talked of his marriage and the tribal law, Mulga was reminded of tales he had heard of the dangers of marrying 'the wrong meat', and the punishment for those who ignored the ancient tribal customs.

Early next morning they were off before the sun rose. After a few miles they crossed a road running west, a faint track that was really an old bullock wagon track, unused for years. Bindi said, 'This will be the last road that we will see until we get back.' Now they rode over a trackless waste of drab grey stunted trees and dry wire and spear grass. This country, unfenced and unused, was left to nature. If cattle or brumbies ventured into this dry, waterless desert they became trapped. The water that might lie in shallow depressions for a few days would dry up, the animals could not find their way back to the permanent waters, so they died out here, their bleached white bones scattered amid the stunted trees and dry grass.

All morning they rode; if they were lucky they would cross the desert before dark. They knew that on the other side were some big creeks that flowed east after the rain. They would be full of water this time of the year. At ten o'clock Bindi stopped the horses and they dismounted, resting for a while, taking a drink from the water-bags they carried around the necks of their horses, and rolling a smoke. In every direction were stunted trees, dry wire grass and ant beds that stood like gravestones in the dead dry landscape. Not even a bird or dingo moved out here. Sometimes there would be a round bare patch of claypan ground where not even the wire grass grew. The ground was littered with the rotted termite-eaten remains of trees. It looked to Mulga as though there was a battle between the stunted trees and the termites. The termites seemed to be winning; the ghostly shapes of their mounds were everywhere.

By midday they pulled up. There was no water for the horses but enough to boil the billy. They unpacked and unsaddled the horses, seeking what shade they could. They guessed they were now more than halfway across the desert; they could see a dark, bluish line that stretched across the horizon ahead. Beyond this range of hills lay their goal. They were sure they would find water in one of the creeks beyond the desert. And in the hills, they knew, were springs and rock holes that would be full after the rain.

After their rest they caught fresh horses and kept heading for the line of hills that gradually grew larger and seemed to stretch forever in each direction. Nothing moved in the never-changing landscape through which they rode, this level flat grey expanse of ant beds and stunted trees. A couple of times they pulled the horses up to spell them, pouring some of the precious water into their upturned hats for the horses they rode. The others would have to wait until they reached the creeks ahead.

By late evening the horses following Bindi veered off to the left and began trotting. As Mulga cantered up to turn them back, they began to whinny. Mulga decided they must be able to smell water. 'Let's follow the horses for a while!' he called to Bindi. Within a few hundred yards the horses found an oasis in the desert, a round depression about the size of a football field covered in a layer of lush green grass, amid giant antbeds eight feet high, built like miniature cathedrals. A fresh clear bubbling spring gurgled to the surface. As the horses reached the water and drank their fill, the men dismounted and lay on their stomachs, dipping their faces into the cool water. Up ahead they could see the hills, their colour now turned from blue to red, and they could make out the place they would head for to get through the range. They decided to camp at the oasis for the night. It was close to their destination; tomorrow they would be able to leave the horses here, ride on and take Comet – if he was there – and return here easily in one day.

They hobbled the horses and set them loose to eat the sweet grass. They noticed a few cattle tracks and knew the creeks were close by; most cattle would never stray far from permanent waters. After dark, as they lay in their swags, they made plans for tomorrow. They had a good idea of just where Comet was being held beyond the line of the red hills, and were sure that by tomorrow they would have him back. They knew that beyond the hills lay rugged canyons. It would be hard on the horses, climbing through narrow gorges and winding tracks mostly used by wallabies and dingoes.

Presently they heard a few cattle come to drink; their shapes were dark against the moonless sky. A deep lowing told them that an old scrub bull was approaching. These were cattle that had not been mustered for years. Some had never seen a man, and in the night they had no fear of him. Although this unfenced country was part of a vast cattle empire, it was never mustered, just left to the scrubbers and brumbies. All the country right up to the range was held by Black Rock and another station to the west.

As Mulga and Bindi made their plans they decided they would take Sandy's rifle with them, secured beneath Bindi's saddle flap. They would get up really early tomorrow, before dawn. Although neither of them carried a watch, waking was no problem. Like most bushmen, they had an instinctive awareness of time. They also marked its passage by the moon and stars in the sky as they rose and set, while daybreak was like an alarm clock to them. So they turned in for the night.

Next morning, as Bindi, bridle in hand, went searching for his horse in the dim light of the stars, Mulga, unhobbling his own horse, heard a loud snort and a bellow followed by much cursing from Bindi. Walking around a huge antbed, Bindi had come face to face with the old scrub bull, sleeping peacefully in the oasis. He'd walked straight into him. Man and bull each got the fright of their lives. Mulga, realising what had happened, doubled up with laughter as Bindi returned leading his horse and still cursing. Mulga told Bindi that if he'd managed to put his bridle on the bull, he would have had to ride it instead of his horse. For years they would both remember that morning and the old scrub bull. Now, mounted up in the reddish gloom of dawn, they headed for the hills.

As soon as they came out of the desert the country changed. Open flats lay before them and soon they came upon a creek with a cool, clear waterhole overhung by ti-trees and eucalypt. They saw many cattle and soon they heard the whistle and snort of a brumby stallion as he pawed the ground, watching them and whinnying as he raced to keep his mares together as they rode past. The grass grew lusher as other creeks were crossed. They came upon another, lone brumby stallion, not yet strong enough to have gained his own herd of mares. It was survival of the strongest out here; the young and not so robust stallions would sometimes wander forever on their own.

Again the country became different: low stony ridges between the hills, mulga trees and spinifex. The hills seemed to close in on them, with no visible gaps in the high boulder-strewn slopes. They kept riding over loose stone and red earth, heading for what looked like a sheer cliff. It looked impassable.

The two men dismounted and rested their horses for a while, rolling smokes and going over their plan. Bindi told Mulga that farther along they would find a pad, mainly used by wallabies and dingoes, that headed up to the cliff and wound around. Climbing upwards towards the cliff wall, riding a zig-zag path, they reached the base of the sheer cliff wall, where they dismounted once again. Along the base of the cliff was the clear, well used animal trail following around the curving rock face. Bindi again headed off, leading his horse now, for the track was just a narrow ledge that followed the cliff face. Below were piles of jumbled loose rock balancing on the steep slopes, as if threatening to topple and crash down to the foothills below. As they rounded a curve, they saw before them, revealed for the first time, a narrow opening in the sheer cliff face, a gap just wide enough to allow maybe a loaded packhorse to pass through. They walked between this narrow opening and came out behind the cliff wall, then stood silent, staring at the sight stretched out before them. It was a different world from the desolate landscape left behind on the other side of the hills.

Below them lay a vista of blue and purple hills and gorges. They could see the sunlight sparkling on miniature waterfalls, glistening as they fell to the valley floor. Silently they studied the scene below for movement of man: there was none. They watched a water lizard sunning itself. Seeing movement above, it dived into a rock hole halfway up the slope. They mounted again and rode into the maze of rocky canyons below where Forklift always held his horses. Bindi pointed to the north. Ten miles away stood the dilapidated homestead of Forklift, hidden by hills that seemed to change colours every few moments in the sunlight.

They reached the valley floor. Small creeks ran from most of the gorges, streams of crystal clear water flowing into a deeper, wider creek that followed the foothills in a meandering path across the valley bottom. Riding on, they reached the narrow mouth of one gorge where rails had been erected across the entrance. It seemed to stretch and widen out as it ran back farther into the hill. Mulga and Sandy watered their horses at the entrance to the gorge, then walked to the sliprails. They knew that they had come to the right place.

8

Behind the sliprails they saw the tracks of horses. A heap of manure, piled up high, told them a stallion was inside. They replaced the sliprails then rode into the gorge. Grass here was plentiful and as they rounded a bend where the country opened out, they came face to face with a herd of horses.

Startled by the unexpected sight of the men, the horses took fright, throwing their heads into the air as they wheeled and raced away. Then Mulga and Bindi saw Comet. They approached him as he emerged from the mob with his neck arched, snorting and stomping. Then, whinnying, he raced back to his mares, herding them close together. By now Mulga had galloped around the herd and now he and Bindi approached the mob from both sides, talking as they rode and calling to Comet. Both men were smiling, they had found Comet at last. As they grew closer, Comet snorted and stamped again. About thirty yards from the herd they stopped. As they continued to talk to Comet, he would come closer to the men, then race back to the herd and put them together again. Then he again ventured closer, smelling the horses and the men. At last Mulga reached out so that Comet could smell his outstretched hand. He gave a knowing, low whinny, and soon Mulga, still on horseback, began to rub him under the jaw and behind the ears.

While Bindi held the mares together Mulga, still talking to Comet and patting him, dismounted. He took the bridle from around his shoulder and placed it over Comet's head. As he patted and rubbed Comet all over the horse was once more a pet. He then led him to where Bindi sat. Together they patted and talked to Comet, telling him what a good horse he was. They were overjoyed to have their favourite horse back.

As it was getting on they decided to have a quick meal near a small rock hole not far away. Mulga saddled up Comet and led him off. At first he began to pigroot, but soon settled down on reaching the water. Comet's tail had always been neat and flowing when he was at Red Hills; now it was knotted and long. Mulga took his pocket-knife and began to run it through the knotted tail, cutting off the long end with one swipe from the blade. The mane was soon pulled and straightened out as well. Once more Mulga and Bindi admired the Comet of old: flowing tail, arched neck, flaring nostrils. Comet was tied to a stunted tree and hobbled while Bindi made tea. Quickly the men ate their meagre lunch of johnny-cakes and corn beef, washing it down with tea from their quart pots. A few minutes' rest and they were eager to be gone from here. They would feel much safer on the other side of the hills. Now they had Comet back they had no wish to meet up with Forklift or his mate.

As they mounted up, Bindi suggested that it might be a good idea to take the mares with them and turn them loose over the hills among the brumby herds. Maybe that would teach Forklift a lesson, he said. 'Okay,' said Mulga as he swung aboard Comet, who went up in the air like a rocket and began to buck. Mulga gave a loud 'Yahoo!' kicked Comet in the gut and slapped his shoulder with the reins. Comet gave one more buck then threw up his head and galloped away. Mulga gave him his head for a while, then wheeled him around and came back at full gallop to where Bindi waited. Comet slid to a halt, chafing at the bit. He would be quiet now he had his usual little buck. A child would have been able to ride him.

Mulga decided to ride in the lead in case the mares wanted to gallop. Bindi, leading their spare horse, would keep the tail going. At the opening to the gorge Mulga pulled both sliprails to the ground. Maybe Forklift and his mate would think that the horses had rubbed down the rails and escaped. After the horses had walked over the rails Mulga called to Bindi to put up one end of the top rail, to make it look as though the horses had broken loose on their own. Bindi was careful where he trod, not wanting to leave boot prints. He lifted the sliprail and put it in place, then remounted without taking two steps for the whole business, and walked the horse over his boot prints. It was important not to leave any plain track that

Forklift and his mate could follow. Mulga, following the tracks they had made coming into the valley, rode ahead. The mares following them would wipe out any trace of their coming.

When they arrived at the cleft in the rock, Mulga dismounted and led Comet through. The mares were wary at first but soon followed Bindi. Not wanting to leave any trace of boot tracks, he tied his bridle around the spare horse's neck as he rode through the gap. The old horse followed. It was much easier going down the hill and they soon reached the bottom. Again they followed the same track they had used coming in, until they reached the river flat before the desert began. Mulga stopped the mares downstream. Along the bank of a deep sandy creek a lone brumby stallion stamped and snorted. He trotted and raced around Bindi, then came around to where Mulga held the leading mares. Mulga told Bindi they would turn the mares over to the stallion, he could have them. Getting behind the horses he said: 'You cut off when we start them up and head for the oasis. I'll give them all a good start downstream. I hope they mix with the brumby herds and that Forklift never sees his mares again.'

With the startled brumby stallion racing excitedly in and out of the herd, Mulga kept going downstream, then headed off into the desert to the oasis, where Bindi already had a fire going. It was now late evening and they would have to camp here again tonight. Comet, blowing and sweating from his hard gallop, was unsaddled, and with side-line and hobbles he was let loose to feed with the other horses.

They carried the pack bags back to the shade of a huge termite mound that cast a long shadow from the sun. It was a few hours before sundown. Contented and pleased with a job well done, they drank tea and prepared a curry, and hoped that Forklift's mares were still galloping and had mixed with the brumby herds.

Forklift would have to come out into the desert to cut their track, and if he did they had nothing to fear. They had not stolen any horses. Forklift's mares had simply got loose and wandered over the hills, and like a lot of station horses before, had mixed with the brumbies.

As they relaxed in the shade, seeing the shadow of the antbed lengthen, they watched Comet as he fed. He was now getting on in years – it was some time now since he had raced. His real value now was in breeding; many of his foals had become top stock horses and brought high prices when sold. Bindi himself owned some mares that ran on Red Hills. He and Sandy were always selling horses. Over the last few years Comet had made a name for himself. His progeny were well in demand as strong, quiet stock horses. Bindi had even bought himself a horse brand, which he stamped on his foals. Mulga had often noticed, when he and Bindi mustered together on Red Hills, that Bindi would always refer to it as 'My Country'.

Mulga still owned no horses, but at Red Hills he would always claim certain horses as if they were his own, and used them in the muster.

After they had eaten they lay in their swags and talked, watching a satellite weave a path across the sky. Then Bindi began to tell stories of the stars, and Mulga listened as he explained their origin in Dreamtime legends. They talked of how man had left his track upon the moon and spaceships now travelled in the endless void called space. Everything that had moved since the dawning of first light seemed to have left a track. From the tracks of animals etched deep into the rocks, millions of years old, to the freshly made track left upon the moon by man.

To Bindi the history of this barren red brown land was told in the creeks and rivers, hills and ranges where the Rainbow Serpent left his track, and from barefoot prints in the desert where man still walked with spear and waddy and hunted as his ancestors did, handing down their legends by word of mouth. And written in the stars was how the white man had walked upon moon dust and come back to earth. Bindi and Mulga talked about the cultures of the tribes, black and white, the beliefs of stone-age people and the progress made by science. Both knew that understanding was the only answer to differences. They felt sure that progress and time would wait for no-one. The world was changing rapidly. Adaptation was the key to survival, for people, animals, everything that lived. Mulga firmly believed that only those that adapted to the changing world would survive, like the forest that had grown and disappeared long before man lived in a house or cut down the first tree. Now another grew in its place, more adapted to the changing times.

As they talked about these things that night, in the wilderness miles from any road or station homestead, they wondered at the oasis itself, surrounded by the harsh dry tract of land. They knew that in a few weeks or months the oasis would disappear, its springs would cease to flow, the grass would dry out and blow away. Then, until the next rainy season, the oasis would become a red bare piece of claypan ground and giant antbeds. What lay beneath the surface of this desert, they did not know. The water must come from some giant, overfull underground supply, but next year there might not be a spring of water here – unless heavy rains fell and the giant underground reservoir was refilled. From the direction of the hills they heard the howl of a lone dingo, but there came no answering call, only the sound of hobble chains as the horses fed. Sometimes they heard Comet whinny as he called to his mares. Again there was no answer. 'I hope the mares have scattered with half a dozen brumby herds now,' Bindi said.

At last they lay silent, until Mulga heard the sound of an old scrub bull as he headed for the water. 'If that's the same old bull again, mate,' he told Bindi, 'you'd better get your bridle, you might catch him this time.' Bindi's answer was a torrent of abuse about smart-arse Murris and bloody scrub bulls that slept near antbeds. Mulga had already pulled the blanket over his head and was dozing off to sleep before Bindi finished his abuse. He was well pleased with the day's work, and smiled as he heard Comet whinny once more, missing his harem but safely sidelined. He could not stray tonight.

Before the first streaks of red appeared in the eastern sky next morning they were miles into the desert, Bindi now riding Comet in the lead. They reached the road by ten o'clock. The horses, now heading home, were walked then trotted for a few miles at a time. Just before sundown they made camp near water, away from the road. Bindi remarked that they only had enough tucker for breakfast, but they would be home tomorrow. Tired and eager to get another early start, they went to bed with the birds.

When Bindi awoke, there was a waning moon in the east. He called to Mulga, and they headed for home by the light of the stars and that pale moon. The horses were eager to be home, and by the first sign of piccaninny dawn they reached their own boundary fence. They found a strainer post where they undid the wires and the horses walked through onto Red Hills once again. Heading for the windmill they rode across the country, and were soon covering the last few miles to the homestead. As they approached the house, Sandy came out, waving his arms excitedly when he saw Comet in the mob. Then the horses were turned loose in the paddock for a well earned rest while Comet was kept in the yard to be patted and fondled by Sandy, acting like some little kid who had just been given his first pony. After a good long shower and shave, Mulga and Bindi made their way to the kitchen, where Sandy had prepared thick steaks, gravy, bread and butter. With feet under the table once again they ate hungrily, and afterwards slept until almost sundown.

That night, Sandy told them that Mary had given birth to a daughter a few days before. She would be home in a few weeks with someone to help her around the house and with the fowls and milkers. And she would have company now when Sandy went droving. Sitting on the verandah, Sandy produced a couple of bottles of rum and they celebrated the birth of his daughter and the return of Comet. While Mulga and Bindi were away, Sandy told them, he had handled three new horses. Tomorrow they would ride them for the first time. But tonight nothing mattered.

Sandy also spoke of his ambition to buy Seven Mile, the property that ran along his top boundary fence. It was much bigger than Red Hills, but for years it had been badly managed by the drunken old bloke who owned it. His wife had run off years ago and he seemed to have no real interest in his property. The fences were falling down, the waters were not maintained. And now it was about to come on the market.

The years had passed swiftly since the three of them had helped themselves to the herds of untamed and unbranded cattle that roamed the unfenced pastures of Mulga Downs. Things were very different these days. Now Sandy had no need to make profits from his neighbour's unbranded beasts. Over the years he had culled his herds and now ran the best quality cattle in the district. He had continued droving for years and had saved much of the profit he made from his cattle sales. Now he had the money to purchase Seven Hills. He spoke to Mulga and Bindi in more detail about his future plans. After mustering and branding his own herd he had lined up a lot of droving mobs for the coming year, including some for Mulga Downs. Bindi and Mulga would have to work one droving plant. But before that he wanted them to walk about three hundred head of his own fat cattle to the railhead. Sandy also told them that he would have to get one of them to look after Red Hills if he bought out his neighbour, as he and Mary would most likely live in the big old homestead at Seven Mile. The place would take a good deal of fixing, but it was on the main road and the mail truck called once a week. It was also connected to the town by telephone. The property itself was much better country than Red Hills and would be able to carry twice the number of cattle.

Their talk spun off into reminiscence as they talked on about days gone by. They spoke of the busters they'd had off bolting horses, being chased by scrub cattle, the cattle rushes in the night ... Of times of drought and the good seasons when the land was a paradise. They recalled bare-knuckle fights, big sprees in town, wild pub brawls. Looking back, it seemed that even in the darkest days there had always been something to laugh at, even oneself.

As the morning star rose in the sky they drained the last bottle of rum and staggered off to bed, with Mulga warning Bindi once again of the dangers of trying to bridle a scrub bull in the dark.

9

In a few weeks Mary and the children returned, together with Mary's cousin, who was about her own age, to help her. Her name was Anne. She was tall, slim, easygoing and good company. A bit of a larrikin, in fact. She had been divorced, and had no children. Anne settled into the bush life as if born into it.

Soon the men finished mustering and Bindi, Mulga and a youngster from the town headed for the railhead and trucking yards with three hundred cattle, while Sandy stayed home breaking in more horses. In two weeks they arrived in town and trucked the cattle to the big city saleyards where they were bought for big prices.

Later that year Sandy brought a large mob of cattle from farther out where the season was dry. Once more he and Mulga and the team of men headed out to take delivery of the herd. Bindi was not with them; he had told them he would be busy doing something else and could not come. Before the previous droving trip had finished, Bindi had told Mulga it was time to go and claim his tribal wife. Again he mentioned the importance of the marriage to 'the right meat', the proper one for him.

Sandy drove his cattle east towards the more settled areas. Soon after starting off he returned to Red Hills, leaving Mulga to take the herd onward. The beasts were sold for a huge profit at the saleyards. The horses they used were also sold for big prices. There were now many horses on Red Hills and like the cattle their numbers had to be controlled. Sandy never overstocked his station, he tried to have quality rather than quantity, and now this policy was starting to pay big dividends. While Sandy headed for home, Mulga, chequed up once more, set off for the city. There he stayed for a year, trying to find something intangible, still searching for answers. Once again he watched the flow of human torrents from suburban trains and buses, jostling in mad haste to beat the factory siren or office clock. Sometimes on the train there would be one hundred people in a carriage. Not a word between them, all silently staring into their newspapers or into space. Their faces told stories of the young, expectant and hopeful or else of dreary resignation to another week of drudgery; unable, unwilling to make changes, their lives lay charted like maps, governed by the clock.

Best of all were the small children. After only a few moments, even though they had never seen each other before they communicated with each other through laughter. They brought smiles to the other dreary faces on the train.

Sometimes Mulga would sit in the crowded city streets where the people swarmed like ants. In this crowded city he sometimes felt a loneliness he never knew in the bush. He had tried to explain this once to a friend. Amid a thousand people he felt alone for the first time in his life. Yet out in the bush, a hundred miles or more from the nearest town, he could never feel alone. Sometimes there were two or three people to talk to, but sometimes he spent weeks alone. When he first felt loneliness in the city, he could not explain his feelings. Later he reasoned they were caused by the hundreds of thousands of people coming and going, more people than he had ever imagined in a lifetime in the bush – yet not one face did he recognise. This, Mulga now knew, was what people described as loneliness. To him the bush with its solitude was never lonely. But here upon these crowded streets he sometimes felt the loneliest man in the world.

Mulga found work on building sites. It was sometimes hard, sometimes easy. He would sit in bars boozing and listening to the men talk about how they made money on the side. He was also employed in the meat works as a casual labourer. Hundreds of mostly long-haired workers lined up each day for work at the abattoirs. One morning the employment officer called out for a stockman. Mulga raised his hand, the only one there. He was amazed when he heard a couple of long hairs talking to each other. 'What *is* a stockman?' one of them asked. 'I don't know,' said the other, as Mulga headed to the office to sign on. It seemed they had no idea where those cattle and sheep came from that kept thousands in work.

On that occasion Mulga spent a couple of days a week in the easiest job he ever had, just hunting up the cattle to fill the killing pen. Other days he was engaged as a knife hand, trimming meat, or sweeping and hosing the floors. Even here every half hour they pulled up for a rest and a smoke. And almost every day after payday, quite early someone would walk through the plant saying that a meeting was being held, a few words from the union bosses. (Who all seemed to talk with a foreign accent.) Then there would be a show of hands from the workers. They always seemed to be intimidated by the union bosses, watching to see who raised their hands before seeing which way they would vote. Always supporting the majority. They seemed frightened to speak out and voice their own opinions, and if someone did speak his mind, he was always talked down by the union bosses. After a while Mulga came to realise that the day after payday was also mid-week race day in the city. And some workers, after voting for stop work for the day, would pack away their knives, pull out their racing form guides and head for the racetrack. Next day, broke again, most of them would return to work as normal.

Even though Mulga had never earned such high pay, he knew he could never settle down to city life. Rushing to catch trains and buses, always paying for something. In the bush the stockman paid no rent nor worried about food unless it was in short supply. These things were supplied, they came with the job. There was no need to collect the weekly wage, there was nowhere to spend it. The stockmen drew their wages, and sometimes they left them untouched for months until they headed for town to bust their cheques on women, booze and betting. Then it was back to the bush again. In the city it was strange to be finished with work each day before the sun went down, to sit and watch television – never seen in the bush – and spend weekends drinking and gambling.

Saturday at the races. Mulga knew that if you wanted to meet other people from the bush then the racetrack was the most likely place they would be when in the city. Here was the jostling crowd around the bookmakers, placing bets. The horses, their coats groomed and glistening as they paraded, the sharp-faced jockeys in glistening silks in all colours of the rainbow. The women were like the horses, groomed, sleek and parading in the latest fashions. The wizened weasel-faced urgers handing out the tips. 'It's a cert' they tell you from the corners of their mouths, always on the move, flitting through the crowd, dodging creditors as the horse they tipped finishes last. They reminded Mulga of wild ducks that would never settle. On race days Mulga met people from Sandy's and Bindi's country. He learned that Sandy had bought out his neighbour on Seven Mile. He also learned that Bindi now had a wife.

One thing Mulga noticed as he roamed the city streets was that the Aborigine was always at the bottom of the ladder. In city parks he saw them drinking wine and metho, hopelessness and despair etched upon their faces. On the weekends the paddy wagons pulled into the pubs and loaded up with their human cargo, whether they were drunk or not. It was enough to be there and black. The police tally sheets showed they had done their work. Of course Mulga had seen the same procedures carried out in a dozen outback towns; at weekends the gaols were full of Aborigines. No whites, unless a murder was committed. It was a crime to be black and standing around near a pub when the police wanted to reach the tally of arrests for the week or month. The policeman's wife who did the cooking for the gaol received big money for each meal – usually a billy of weak black tea and some jam sandwiches. Most Aborigines had no bail money. Then on Monday twenty of them would be charged for being drunk, and some given a week's gaol.

Even under these conditions a lot of Murris rose above their would-be suppressors. Mulga himself had been down but never out many times himself. But he had never despaired even in the darkest days. He knew it was a disadvantage being black in a white-dominated society. Yet he knew both his own capabilities and those of others and never felt he had to look up to anyone in his work as a stockman or drover, or in many other jobs. He knew good people both white and black; he envied no man but set his own goals. He knew that things never happened on their own. People made things happen. He often liked to boast that if he did anything he did it properly; even when drinking he never let anything interfere with it.

And if he wanted something he worked till he had it. He believed in himself, not in other people. If you wanted something you did not wait for someone else to bring it to you. Some people waited forever for things to happen. He also knew that hope was much better than bitterness and despair.

In the city the characters Mulga met were good and bad, people of all colours and creeds.

One day Mulga thought he would write about how he felt, tell the real stories of the bush and city life he knew. He realised that to talk about these things was not enough; even as the words left your mouth they were gone like the wind, forgotten.

When Mulga had come to the city for the first time he'd been a real country bumpkin. He remembered those early days, standing on some corner with city-wise friends. He remembered looking up, seeing the sign of 'No Standing Anytime'. While his mates stood in front of the sign talking he would edge away, expecting any moment a policeman to appear and ask them to move on. He was as green as the leaves of a wilga tree in the ways of city life. But he learnt fast by watching and listening.

It was not long before Mulga again felt the urge for change. This happened one day as he walked the crowded streets with peak hour shoppers moving like ants in every direction. As he sat on a bus stop bench, once again he felt terribly alone amid the rushing crowd. It was overwhelming. Within a few days he was on a train heading west, back to the bush, to a life that sometimes brought solitude, but never loneliness. The train left in the late evening, rushing past almost deserted suburban railway stations, rows and rows of identical houses, and empty streets. Then Mulga saw vacant blocks and along the railway line the grass got longer and greener. He wondered how many cattle or sheep could be grazed around here. The lush grass was wasted while in the drought hundreds of thousands of stock starved outback.

Soon the train climbed the coastal ranges, and as Mulga looked at the lights from the suburban and farming towns he was reminded of a bushfire he had once seen from a ridge at night, the tree-tops alight after the bush fire had raced through the scrub, five hundred miles inland. Gradually the township lights became fewer, just pin-pricks of light from the valleys below. The dark shapes of the mountain ranges loomed above the tops of tall straight trees and on one side there was a sheer descent to the valley below. On the other side were rugged rocky cliff walls. You could feel the swaying of the carriage and hear the iron wheels grating as they fought for traction on the railway as the train slowly laboured up the range, turning and twisting through the tunnels. After hours of snail-pace progress to the top of the range, it was as though the train at last burst through a big boundary fence: the ranges, now left behind, stood like a barrier to the ocean and the bustling city life below. Ahead the rich farming land stretched out, and beyond lay the wide unfenced pastures, the sheep and cattle empires of the open plains and the mulga forest. Flooded channel country and the red spinifex, sandhills and stony deserts.

The land where horizons never ended was Mulga's country, the land of feast or famine, from the muddy brown waters that spread for miles in good seasons, leaving behind the richest grazing land of them all as they receded. The waving Mitchell grass plains, where the grass grew stirrup-high as stockmen rode in years of plenty. In drought this same country became the devil's playground, all waters dried up, the grass withered and dead as the land turned cracked and barren. In the searing heat of summer the hot winds stirred the willy-willies that seemed to dance across the parched, sunburned ground. The heatwave shimmering in the glaring sunlight created mirages in the sky. Burning, shifting sandhills with spinifex clinging to their sides. Then the ground became littered with the carcases of dead stock, while those who still lived, walking skeletons, foraged for a blade of grass or fallen leaves. Around the drying waterholes, stuck deep in mud, animals faced a slow and painful death, while the hawks and crows circled overhead. Farther out still, day turned to night as big clouds of sand and dust blocked out the sun and blew for days. Mulga knew well this land of contrast, he'd seen it all from horseback as he wandered across the country. He also knew that after drought came flooding rains, the land once more became a paradise and the years of hardship were forgotten by the people who lived out there.

★

It's the people you remember when you take the long, slow ride inland, sometimes for a day or more. Monotony is broken as the wheels clack and the carriages sway. The train seems to sing a different tune as it heads inland. People try to sleep, blinds pulled down even though there's only darkness outside the window. But sleep is hard to come by when you travel second-class; there's always some yahoo stoned on yarni or pissed to the eyeballs. He keeps people awake all night, raving and singing, laughing at his own jokes, loud-mouthed and brash. Then, just as dawn is breaking and you want to use the toilet, hard up against the door you'll find a yahoo crashed out. With daylight and breakfast people begin to stir. Two women start talking. They've never met before. One is going to see her daughter, the other has a grandson who lives out west. They soon discover they both know someone who lives nearby, and someone else related to someone who knew someone's cousin on their mother's side, or maybe it was on the uncle's side ... Relentlessly, like the clacking of the train wheels, the talking continues.

In the next carriage two old Murri mates who boarded the train during the night sit staring into space as Mulga walks past and says good-day. In their ragged clothes, with a week's stubble of black-grey beard and tustled uncombed hair, they might be sleeping, Mulga thought, except for their wide-open eyes. They didn't answer him. Later he walks past again – they recognise him this time and greet him warmly. These two men, young in years yet so old in looks, tell Mulga their story. He knew them both: they were good stockmen when he last saw them, but for the past few years they had become used to city life, existing on the dole. They told Mulga they had fallen on hard times, from which they were trying to escape. They had been sentenced to gaol for unpaid fines.

Mulga knew that unjust gaol terms were handed out to Murris for even minor crimes, when whites were always allowed bail. Even in the outback courts, he had seen unjust sentences handed out, always by the white judges or magistrates. Especially drink driving charges. Mulga had seen young Aborigines, first offenders, fined a thousand dollars, disqualified from driving for years, their lives left in tatters. Next in court might be some white man on his fourth or fifth offence, pleading leniency, his lawyer declaring what a good man was he. (Even as the man was shaking for want of a drink.) He should be given a chance, the magistrate decreed, handing down the sentence: a hundred and fifty dollar fine and the loss of his licence for three months. Contrasted to what amounted to a death sentence for the young Aborigine.

In gaol, these two Murris had mixed with hardened criminals – but they talked about the humorous things that had happened, not the brutality. It seemed as though their defence against misfortune was to laugh. Released from gaol, they floundered in the city like fish out of water and ended up sleeping on park benches with newspapers for a blanket. Then plonk, followed by metho or 'the white lady' as it was sometimes called. They became part of the goomies mob, wandering the streets, begging for the price of a bottle, a feed, a bed. Mulga himself had seen those mobs of homeless goomies, black and white, scrounging in garbage bins, unwashed, wearing rags. Colour knew no boundary when it came to the down and out.

Now at last these two Murris were heading home to the bush, trying to beat the grog, to regain some dignity. They told Mulga they had no idea how they'd got on the train during the night. One of them had tried to open the exit door and walk out. He laughed. 'I must of thought the train was going too slow and I'd walk ahead and get home faster,' he said. The other mate said, 'I had no idea where I was all night. I heard this noise and felt this swaying and thought I was in a car. The conductor took the bottle from us and now we're sick – sober for once.' Mulga offered to talk to the guard and see if he could get back their grog, but they said, 'No, don't bother, it's only a bottle of goom.'

As the train took Mulga farther west, his thoughts turned to the differences that existed in the lifestyles of the Murris in the outback. Whenever he was employed at some big station, he and about ten other stockmen, black and white, worked and ate together as a matter of course, did the same work and were paid the same wages. But in the deep north, Aborigines from the church missions seemed to have learned nothing about the real world, except to say 'thank you', 'amen' and little else. Any mention of fair working conditions, equal pay or the right to speak out was taboo to the so-called Christian missionaries. Anyone who questioned their ideas were thought of as shit stirrers. If any Murri 'got cheeky', as the missionaries would say, he would be bundled off to Palm Island or another penal institution, while pious prayers were said. It had not been easy, within an illiterate white racist society, for the other Murris to win equal pay and the right to work and live where they chose. Mulga and Bindi had been lucky to escape the oppressive church missions.

Sitting there in the railway carriage, Mulga recalled one old Murri who was known as 'Ringer', a stockman, who had once told him his personal story of prejudice and first contact with the white man's world. Ringer's mother was a tribal woman, his father Irish – he managed the station where his children were born and bred. Whenever a stranger rode up, the kids were told to go bush. Their bearded Irish father would greet all strangers from the doorway, where on either side he kept two loaded rifles in case they were government men with an interest in taking his dark-skinned kids away to the mission. Ringer was sure that if any stranger had tried to take him or his twelve brothers and sisters away, they would have been buried out there, deep beneath the mulga scrub.

When Ringer was five, he told Mulga he was taken in a sulky, which was the mail service, thirty miles to the nearest bush town to attend school. He still remembered very well his brief taste of education. He was the only Murri at the school, and was picked on and fought with every white kid, some twice his size. They ganged up on him and as a result he learned only two things at that school: either to fight good or run fast. His father rode to town five days after Ringer had left home and found him in bed in the house where he was staying with an old Murri couple, his eyes so battered and swollen he couldn't see. His father took one look at him then went to the school and abused the teacher and his so-called civilised pupils. Then, putting a hat on Ringer's head and shading his eyes with a handkerchief, he lifted him up behind his saddle and they rode home together.

But Ringer *had* learned to run and to fight better than most, and when he grew up he achieved one of his secret desires, returning to that small town and beating the shit out of his tormentors from those five schooldays, one by one. He claimed it was one of the greatest pleasures in his life.

Ringer was getting on in years now. Today, he told Mulga, it seemed that the fight for equal rights was being won, with the Murris themselves now wanting a self-imposed segregation. They were fed up with being led up dry gullies by do-gooders, by greenies urging them to help with land conservation claims – not for the benefit of the Murris but for their own self-interests. These conservationists cared about the welfare of animals and plants; they gave no thought to the health or housing conditions of the Murris they hoped to hide away in their conservation parks. The Aborigines themselves should make their own claims on parks and sacred sights, Ringer told Mulga, so that they could retain their culture. But nothing could be achieved without education. 'Are we to be forever ruled by the past, with no thought for the future?' Ringer asked. He thought Aboriginal culture could be retained, but in this ever-changing world only those who were willing to adapt would succeed. If the present is alive, he said, then the past can only be a cherished memory for some – not so cherished by others. There was no place today for stone-age lifestyles.

And these were some of the thoughts, encounters and memories that occurred in the course of Mulga's long, slow journey west.

10

Back in the bush once more, Mulga was now employed running scrubbers, mustering on the stony plains amid the stunted gydgea trees, river channels and sandhills in the cool winter months. When enough bullocks were in hand for the market, a drover was employed to walk the cattle to the railhead.

Mulga watched the cattle being counted over to the drover, a Murri who was travelling with his family. The two youngest children, just toddlers, rode with their mother in a horse-drawn wagonette. The oldest girl, maybe sixteen, was horse tailer, in charge of forty horses. She would muster the horses and have them back at camp each day before the first red glow of dawn. Every night she would hobble the horses with greenhide straps – and again, before dawn, in the cold damp grass she would catch and unhobble them once more.

Seeing that Aboriginal family reminded Mulga of another encounter he had one day when taking some horses north to grass. Through the dust haze ahead he'd watched as another group of packhorse drovers approached in front of a mob of cattle. As they drew near he saw that one of the riders was carrying something in front of the saddle. To Mulga's amazement he saw it was a baby, perhaps a year old, sitting on a pillow tied to the saddle and held around the waist by its young Aboriginal mother, who wore men's trousers, an old felt hat and riding boots. Both groups pulled up and Mulga talked for a while to the woman. He learned that she did the cooking for the camp and looked after the baby while her two other kids helped to drive the cattle – their saddles were bigger than the riders. They had been on the road for three months.

Across the stock routes of the west, Mulga had seen many women in the camps, driving trucks and wagonettes, horses four in hand, their kids helping with the stock as their mother cooked on the open fire. At night, around the camp fire, by the dim light of a kerosene or carbide lamp, she taught them what little she knew. Yes, he'd seen many women, white and black, with their men and kids, their weather-beaten faces etched deep with lines of care and worry as they battled through. Their nearest supermarket might be two hundred miles away. There was no doctor's surgery, no chemist shop; their medical kit was mostly castor oil, aspros and Vicks. No Avon lady called out here! Kindergarten for the kids was a hundred miles or more of the stock routes of the west, their storybooks told in the tracks of horses, sheep and cattle and all the native animals and birds of this ever-changing land. Out in the bush, sometimes for months on end, these women helped to take stock to railheads for trucking to the coast, to feed a hungry nation, which seemed to think all its food began and ended in the supermarket. It seemed to Mulga and his mates that if they closed down the bush, the city would starve: no meat or vegetables, wool or timber. Yet if all the cities were closed down, the bush and the people who lived in it would survive. Thousands of years of Aboriginal culture was proof of this.

Of all the women he'd met who worked with the droving mobs, Mulga had never forgotten his admiration for the young mother who carried her baby on the saddle pommel in the packhorse drovers' camp. And he thought that if ever he wrote a book it would contain people like her, the real heroes of the West.

Now, as the station stockmen watched the drover with his family and five hundred bullocks head for the railway trucking yards two hundred miles away, they themselves felt restless. Having finished the first round of the muster, they would be heading for town as well – but, unlike the droving family, whose journey would take at least a month, the stockmen would make the journey in a matter of hours over the rough, corrugated road in the station truck.

For this was August, and in Queensland's north-west, the only topic now discussed around the camp fires was the rodeo and mardi gras at Mount Isa. It was often said that Australia stopped for a few minutes each year when the Melbourne Cup was run: this was not true so far as the north-west was concerned. But, come August, for a few days, maybe a whole week, work certainly came to a halt as stockmen and station owners headed for the Isa. Even the drovers with their travelling mobs knew many men would pull out, not wanting to miss the few days each year when the north-west came alive. Sensible bosses would give their stockmen a few days off. Afterwards, most would return to finish the muster. Broke, sore and sorry, they would be happy to be back in the bush earning another big cheque, doing what they liked most: riding horses and chasing stock.

Yet there were some bosses who still expected their stockmen to go on working a seven-day week for months on end, many not even wanting to pay for weekend work. Then the stockmen would simply roll their swags and catch the mail truck to town and the money-hungry boss was left cursing. Some bosses expected men to stay in the bush for a whole year. Their only concerns were the company books of the huge stations they managed, often for overseas landlords, their own status and the welfare of the animals. The stockmen came last on the list of their priorities. Such managers were treated with contempt by their stockmen, who regarded them only as someone who wrote out the cheque when the work was done. Respect from the stockman could only be earned.

And now it was August again and lines of stockmen waited outside station offices while the bookkeepers made up the cheques. Meanwhile, around the stockman's huts they cut each other's hair, polished their R.M. Williams riding boots, put on their best gear and tried to catch the eye of the housemaid or maybe a governess employed at the homestead. Soon the last cheque was made up, with the stockmen studying their statements carefully. Even though some could not read, they could count real good. Then they piled onto the back of the station truck and headed for the Isa and rodeo.

Sprawled among their swags during the long journey over the dirt road, they were soon covered in fine red dust. Silently they urged the truck on faster as the rugged spinifex hills came in view ... miles before they reached the city they could see smoke rising from the tall stack that towered above the Isa and its slag heaps and dusty streets. The smoke and the fumes seemed to hang like a sheet over the town, trying to blot out the weak winter sun. This was the Isa: wide, steep streets, houses perched on the hillsides.

Then they were across the dry, stony creek bed and their first stop was the pub. After months in the bush they breasted the long bar counter, eyeing the barmaids refilling their glasses, meeting other stockmen already half-pissed. And among those other stockmen were Mulga and Bindi, who had met up after arriving in the Isa.

The bars became more crowded still as shift workers arrived from the mine. Many of the miners were former stockmen, most now married, who had moved to the Isa. Still they felt their old longing for the bush and a yarn with old mates. As someone once said, if anyone ever cracked a stockwhip outside the Isa mines, half the men would drop tools and rush out to see what was happening.

To the stockmen, white and black, and the Aboriginal family groups that came to town from the big, far-off cattle and mission stations, accommodation was no problem. They rolled out their swags on verandahs and in backyards or along the creek bank. Around the hills smoke rose from camp fires of a hundred different mobs. Some of the Aborigines from those far-off stations, where they still lived in huge family groups, had come all the way to the Isa loaded into cattle crates on semi-trailers. But travelling rough didn't worry those underpaid workers; their one thought was to enjoy their only holiday of the year, camped around the rodeo ground.

That night, Mulga and a mob of old stockmen mates did the pub rounds, greeting each other as they walked along the crowded streets. 'Hey! There's old Pineapple – Quart-Pot – the Flea – White Horse – Eagle Hawk – Ten-Eighty – Duck Pigeon ...' They hailed each other by a hundred nicknames. It seemed that in the bush most people only knew each other by nicknames. If you asked someone where 'Billy Smith' was, he would shrug and say, 'Don't know him', but if you asked for 'Flour-Bag' or 'Grader', he'd know who you meant immediately. Once given, a tag stuck – it may have been for something a person had once done, or just related to his work. Like 'the Tick': he'd earned his name because he smelled like cattle dip, and it was claimed that when he got on a wild horse or a woman, the only way he could be removed was to spray him with cattle dip – then he would fall off. Now the men greeted a woman called 'Electric Effie', who had earned her name by lighting up the whole town. Even the bosses earned their names: Sugar-Bag, Johnny-cake, Top-Wire, Green-Hide …

They stood on a street corner for a while waving to people and calling out as they went past. A drunken brawl started in the pub behind them and suddenly one bloke came crashing into the street, landing on his back right beside Mulga and his friends. The loser lay for a moment motionless on the pavement. Mulga and the others checked that he wasn't badly hurt, and meanwhile the winner, his courage boosted by victory, stood in the pub doorway shouting what else he would do to his moaning victim if he returned. The loser opened his eyes and shook his head. Skin was peeling from below his left eye, which was already turning blue as Mulga and the others helped him to his feet. He told them he worked on a station farther south, and when they saw he was drinking alone, one of the town blokes, surrounded by his mates, had deliberately picked a fight – and so he'd landed up on the hard footpath.

Through the windows they all heard the laughter of the town hoodlums as they guzzled their beer. 'Let's go in and have a drink,' said one of Mulga's mates. He turned to their new stockman friend, whose damaged eye was swelling rapidly. 'They told you not to come back – let's see if they can throw us all out.' 'Yeh!' said the Tick, who was with them. 'Come with us, Boko.' He instinctively nicknamed the stranger 'Boko' after the story of a famous one-eyed horse.

Into the bar they walked. Ordering drinks, they moved over to the loud-mouthed lout. The town mob eyed the stockmen silently for a while. There were seven in their mob and about ten stockmen, but many more around the bar were friends or relations of the louts. After a few drinks everything seemed to have settled down. Boko was back drinking in the pub the lout had told him not to enter: the stockmen had proved their point.

Then the Tick, sitting closest to the louts, began to exclaim: 'Gee, can you blokes smell that stink? Gawd, what a pong!' Itching for a fight, he looked straight at the lout who had punched Boko. 'It's you, ya unwashed bastard! Ya stink like a maggoty sheep.'

'You talkin' to me, ya little saddle-frigging bastard?' the lout replied. Before he could say another word, the Tick, small and wiry, sprang from his bar stool and landed a king hit on his jaw. The lout crashed to the floor, unconscious. Then the Tick, knowing he had his mates behind him, said bravely: 'If you town bastards want to take your mate's part ya can. I'll have any of ya!' He gave a few shuffles and made shadow-boxing movements. At this, another bloke standing near the Tick gave him a left hook below the ear and the hero collapsed to the floor, his light switched off.

A real brawl started then, with the two instigators lying unconscious. Punches, boots and bar stools flew; for a few moments bedlam reigned. A couple of bouncers employed by the hotel stood and watched, waiting for the odds to swing in their favour before trying to restore order. The longer the fight, the more louts and stockmen would be put out. Apart from a few swipes with bar stools and kicks in the guts, they were now mostly using their fists. Then about eight police came through the door. The wise old sergeant leading them had seen a thousand pub brawls in his day. He blew his whistle and called for the action to stop. It did: everyone was exhausted. The sergeant wanted to know what started the fight. No-one answered because no-one could remember. While the sergeant chastised them all, the louts and stockmen looked at their mates, some unconscious on the floor, others with bleeding mouths and noses, skint knuckles and maybe a cracked rib from a kick in the guts. Then the publican said he would ban them from his hotel if they made any more trouble, and the sergeant threatened to lock them all up until after the rodeo was over if they caused another fight. The police left, and louts and stockmen began to talk and drink with each other. They were now friends. Everyone was happy, especially the publican, listening to the ringing of the cash registers as the men drank on.

And now the talk around all the bars in town was of bucking horses and great horsemen as the miners and stockmen were joined by travelling rodeo riders who followed the rodeo circuit, eking out a living in the toughest sport of all, rewarded for their victories with prize money and paying for their mistakes with bruised or broken bones, living on rump steak one week, diving for mussels the next. Many of the stockmen could hold their own with the rodeo riders, and this was the week they set out to prove it.

One evening, Mulga and Bindi met up with Sandy; together they shared a few quiet drinks as they talked. Sandy, now the owner of two stations, no longer camped or rolled out his swag on some verandah. He stayed in the best hotel and did most of his drinking in the private bars with other station owners and managers. Bindi was now the boundary rider on Red Hills, where he lived with his wife and kids, contented to be on part of his tribal lands. He had never been a heavy drinker like Mulga: for both Bindi and Sandy, there were no more of those all-night sessions of the past. Their lifestyles had changed over the years; only Mulga's way of life remained the same. He still went looking for answers, searching for intangibles. But despite the differences they were still the best of mates. Sandy would always ask Mulga if he was okay for work and so would Bindi.

At the Isa, Bindi camped with other tribal mobs. Around the fire they would talk all night. To most of them the past seemed to hold more than the present or the future, although for many changes for the better were beginning to take place. Some had begun to hope that after the long years of suppression there really was a future for them.

One night Mulga joined them and once again, as they joked about their struggles, he thought these must be the only people on earth who could laugh at misery and injustice. Maybe that was the key to their survival.

Their struggles made Mulga regard episodes such as the Eureka Stockade as a girl guides' picnic. For example, after the war, Aborigines had gone on strike for better wages. The police were then sent to recruit slave labour for the money-hungry graziers. But for the first time they found they could not make any of the Aborigines work. Some of the strikers were taken off to gaol, chained together, singing as they went. Others took to the hills and scratched for an existence trying to mine for minerals. But while the strike lasted they were refused a miner's right to register their claims. The government suppressed all information about this struggle. Eventually, however, news of the strike filtered through to the wharfies in the city, who threatened to place bans on loading the squatters' wool. Then the Murris were set free from the gaols. So they won a fight but lost the battle – without a shot being fired against their white oppressors.

This night, Mulga was told another story. Years ago, an Aboriginal stockman – probably a better stockman and horseman than any of the whites on the station where he worked – entered an outback hotel and asked for a drink. 'We don't serve blacks in here,' the uppity barmaid told him. Then the Murri pulled out a pistol, aimed at the woman's head and squeezed the trigger. The bullet parted her hair and she fainted dead away. The Murri walked around the bar, stepping over her, and helped himself to bottles of rum and whisky, then mounted his horse and headed back for the station. Sick and tired of white attitudes, he took over the station storeroom and a gun battle ensued. Like the famous black warrior Pigeon (who, unlike Ned Kelly, is written about as a murderer rather than a legendary hero), the Murri was killed not by the white enemy, but by one of his own race.

~

It was the rodeo of rodeos in Australia, with the tougher bucking horses from the stations of the north sent to the Isa, where some became bigger stars than the riders themselves. The Isa always drew the best travelling riders because of the horses and the prize money on offer. A win here would keep a rider going with travel and entry money for months.

In the bars they mingled: rodeo riders, stockmen, hard-rock miners and the tribal Aborigines from the stations and the missions, talking in a dozen different dialects. The miners, as well as some old drovers and station men, had come to Australia from every nation on earth, and many talked in their own lingo. Mulga had heard it said that the only two tribes of people not employed in the huge copper and lead mines were the Eskimo and the Red Indian. It was also said that the company had imported one of each to prove people wrong.

Many of the younger stockmen had been talked into nominating for the novice rides; other more experienced stockmen would compete with the pros in the open events in riding, roping, bull-dogging and camp-drafting. Men from the stations had brought in their best stock horses for the pick-up teams that would pick the rider from the back of a bolting or bucking horse and return the horse to the yard. Men like these, as well as the other workers in the yard made the rodeo happen – they were the unsung heroes of the game.

In the bar one evening, Mulga watched as a stockman called Gydgea gave some new chum riders advice about the finer points of riding in rodeo. Gydgea was a top horseman in the bush as well as the rodeo arena. Although he never travelled full time he could hold his own with the best. Soon Gydgea had those new chums sitting on their bar stools marking out imaginary horses, holding the rope halters or bareback rigging and bull ropes. As the novices took this last-minute lesson some overbalanced on their stools and fell to the floor. 'It's all right,' Gydgea said as he lifted one bloke back onto his stool, 'have another go.' So they carried on until Gydgea, not wanting any more interference with his drinking, told the youngsters still trying to spur the bar stools: 'The best advice I can give youse is to keep one leg each side of a bucking horse and your arse in the middle – then you'll never be thrown.'

As Gydgea breasted up to the bar, another half-drunk stockman was giving advice about bull-dogging, showing how he wrestled steers to the ground. He had one of his mates in a headlock and began to apply pressure, twisting his mate's head till at last the victim could stand the pain no longer. Almost choking, he drove his fist into the solar plexis of the bulldogger, who collapsed onto the floor, winded. When he regained his breath he said, 'What ya do that for, ya little bastard?' – 'Ya nearly broke my bloody neck, ya silly bastard,' came the reply.

'All the wildest rides take place in bars the night before rodeo begins,' said a whiskery-faced old drover as he downed his rum in one gulp and called for another. 'I've been travelling for years,' he told Gydgea, 'and I'll tell ya, mate, I've seen a hundred scored on a bucking bull and ninety-nine chalked up on a bucking horse *and* the biggest steer in the world wrestled to the floor in many a hotel bar – and all in five seconds flat. Ya know what,' he went on, turning to Mulga, 'the fastest roping time ever was set last year in this here bar.'

By this time most of the stockmen turned miners who were there drinking with Mulga, Gydgea and the others had decided they would be taking sickies tomorrow for the rodeo. For them, as they watched the horses and cattle buck and spin it would be an escape back to the bush, and the thrills and excitement would help them to endure the coming year in the deep underground mines. Although their wages in the mines were triple those of stockmen, they still treasured their memories of carefree days outback in the mustering camps and on droving trips.

Soon the bars closed and big supplies of grog were taken off by those who would drink the night away. Some, as they emerged from the hotels, were still riding imaginary horses or throwing steers. Most of these would be missing from the arena in the morning when their names were called over the loud speakers. Later in the day they would front up in their fanciest shirts and trousers, many bruised and battered or with the old rodeo limp, claiming they'd been involved in accidents. But the truth was they had already ridden their rodeo the night before.

Around the arena next day gathered the huge crowd of this true multi-cultural city. Only the Aborigines seemed out of place amidst the evidence of prosperity. They were the only losers, aliens in their homeland as they wandered, often barefoot, in the city streets or woke from drunken sleep in the dry river bed. To the white migrants they seemed part of the landscape, like kangaroos. None of the wealth from the great mines had flowed to these traditional owners of the tribal lands. They wandered homeless and disillusioned while day and night their mother earth gave up untold riches that allowed the largely migrant population of this northern city to enjoy a lifestyle undreamed of in their native lands.

That such poverty could exist in one race of people in the midst of all that wealth seemed beyond comprehension. Many people were fond of saying that the Aborigines could not be helped. But after all, there was nothing very smart about digging something from the ground. Could not the Aborigines have negotiated mineral royalties with the overseas buyers of the riches of their land? Once the minerals had all been taken, all that was left was a great big hole.

Mulga thought about these things even in the midst of the rodeo excitement. When all the minerals were mined – and all the land belonging to the huge pastoral leases was laid bare by the over-grazing of imported sheep and cattle – what would happen to the migrants' prosperity then? The rate things were going, Australia's natural resources would not last another two hundred years. It seemed to Mulga that those who exploited the land, both below and above the surface, owed some obligation to the true guardians of that land: at least a decent way of life and proper health standards. He felt sure it was not the right answer for the Aborigines to return to the bush to live in self-imposed segregation. There they were out of sight, out of mind ... until a tourist bus pulled up, when they themselves were exploited, like the land, to benefit the white tourist industry. The camera clicks – 'Smile, Jacky!' A pat on the head – 'You good black fella, you don't complain like those other blacks, wanting money and education. You don't need education out here. Your babies like crawling in the dirt, and the dogs lick out your pots and pans real good. What more do you want? – Oh, look, a kangaroo!'

Imagine, Mulga thought, the outcry from white Australians if all these Aboriginal people moved into the inland towns. What an uproar that would cause from those who claimed the Aborigines could not be helped or educated into the modern age while still retaining their own culture. Yet in the Isa, Mulga saw the clubs of the different nations keeping alive the cultures of the migrants' homelands, even though they had forsaken their own countries for a better way of life. And at the same time, of course, they strove for even better living conditions and higher standards of education.

The time had come for the Aborigines to decide whether they would continue to endure their third-world conditions in segregation or isolation or join the real world of today.

Around a camp fire one night, someone had told a story which Mulga often quoted when he put forward his ideas for the future of his people. This was the story: In the beginning, after God created the earth, all the animals and mankind, he gathered together the tribes, black and white, and gave his orders: 'You go east and multiply – you go south – you north – you west' – until everyone had dispersed. God felt good: right here in Australia was his creation of Paradise. He was just about to return to his kingdom in the sky when he looked behind him. There, still playing on the edge of a billabong, was a small tribe of Murris. God stared at them for a moment then shouted out: 'I forgot all about you fellas! Don't worry – you just wait here until I come back.' Then he disappeared in a cloud of smoke.

Mulga, like many other Murris, had grown tired of waiting. Everyone lived in the present and only those who planned for the future themselves would benefit from it, whether black or white. It was no good waiting for someone else to shape it for them.

This red-brown land was certainly Paradise, Mulga thought, and the only way the Aboriginal people could take a firm hold of a piece of Paradise in the space age was through education. Today the call was for land rights, yet few, black or white, knew what that meant. Mulga was convinced the greatest need of his people was for health and housing – and neither could be achieved without education. So education was the key to open all doors to a sharing of wealth, land rights and the preservation of Aboriginal culture. To Mulga it seemed that his people, screaming for land rights without first ensuring they had obtained education and proper health care and housing, had once more played into the hands of the white man. Once land rights were granted, his people would have played their trump card. Their further pleas would be empty. They would have their land – and they would still have the worst health problems in the world. While a few black leaders became rich, the others would gain nothing. For Mulga knew that 'Aboriginal sharing' was a myth in this day and age. Just like the whites, the greedy Aborigines got more, the needy less. The true tribal life was finished forever. Now meat came in a tin, walkabout was by four-wheel drive, the social welfare cheque kept them going.

Yet there were Aborigines who had made the grade unaided, successful in their chosen fields in the modern world, yet still retaining their Aboriginality. They knew that being Aboriginal did not mean sitting in the dust smiling for the tourist dollar, with their children brought up in ignorance of the real world. They had discovered that education was the key. Only by education would the Aborigine ensure his future when land rights were claimed.

Sometimes Mulga pictured a titanic struggle between a Rainbow Serpent and many a man-made gods, looked down on from above by spectators in a spaceship, trying to separate fact from fiction as they watched a big all-in brawl. What were they fighting over – a ruined earth or that one empty seat on the spaceship and a place in the future.

Many changes had been made during the last forty years, but many more needed to be made by all Australians to address the injustices of the past and the present inequality of health, housing, education and work standards. Like the myth of Aboriginal sharing, the white Australian myth of 'a fair go' was equally absurd. The making of this nation has only just begun, Mulga thought as he watched the great crowd gathered for the rodeo and listened to all these people talking in their different lingos as they watched the action or drank and argued around the bars. Multiculturalism: no-one seemed to care what that phrase really meant. If this was multiculturalism in action all around him, why did it work for everyone except the true guardians of the land?

Snorting horses, bellowing cattle, cheering crowds: this was rodeo. Over the next few days, there was much talk of past glories in wild bush rides and the rodeo arena. Old-timers leaning on their walking sticks shook their heads in disgust as they sipped their rum and watched the horses buck off the contestants. 'If only we were young again,' Jam-Tin told another grey-bearded stockman, 'we'd show these blokes how to ride.' Through blurry, faded eyes he watched one horse almost turn inside out as it bucked high, twisting, spinning, kicking out, then dropping its shoulder blade and sucking back as its rider became airborne and headed for the earth. All around the arena they argued about the merits of the horses and their riders. They were all riders, in the grandstand and at the bars.

Mulga and Gydgea walked through the crowd seeking a better vantage point. Everyone seemed to be wearing a cowboy hat – the littlest kids, the miners, the women. For a few days each year even the townsfolk went Western. Shop assistants, bank tellers, barmaids all dressed in Western gear – everyone a cowboy *or* cowgirl. Mulga noticed a family group and recognised the father, a boundary rider from an outback station. His children, nine of them all told, were in steps and stairs from a toddler to teenagers. This man came to town twice each year: once for his wife to give birth and again at rodeo time. He always wore the biggest sombrero, and like their father, every one of the kids wore a sombrero as well. The smallest were hidden under their huge hats. Gydgea, who could always see the funny side of things, turned to Mulga and said: 'See those big hats floating around? Well, don't kick 'em – they've got bloody little kids underneath them.' He added: 'Can't understand why that bastard bothers to buy himself a hat at all when he must spend most of his time in bed with his wife.'

Soon there was a lull in the arena, and Mulga and Gydgea were drawn to a two-up game started by some rodeo rider who'd missed out on his chance for big prize money. A crowd had soon gathered as the call of 'Come in spinner' was heard, periodically drowned out by the loudspeakers from the arena. A curious tourist asked Mulga what was going on as the crowd stooped down all together, as though performing some ancient ritual, then gazed skywards: up then down the heads would go, straining for a glimpse of the two copper pennies tossed into the air. This went on for an hour until a mob of police arrived to warn the illegal penny-worshippers. Ten minutes later, the police safely out of sight, they resumed their worship, and so it went on throughout the day.

After two days and nights of spills, fights and romance, the rodeo was over for another year. The champion wore his ribbon and a grin, while the loser nursed bruises, sprains and sometimes broken bones. But still they would limp on to the next rodeo. There was an old saying: the only way to stop a rider competing was to cut off his head and plant it where he couldn't find it. There was another saying – that the only qualifications for being a bull rider were a pair of spurs and no brains. This might be true for some of them, those who would try to ride a cyclone if they could just get someone to tighten up their bull ropes.

Even before the last horse bucked out of the chute into the arena, some had rolled up their swags and were headed back to the bush; but at sunset many camp fires still glowed around the hills and the rodeo ground. Tomorrow they would all leave town and peace and quiet would return to the arena, the surrounding hills and the creeksides until next year, when

from the tribal lands of the Kalkadoons
from spinifex hills
and stony desert
from the brackish waters
of northern gulf
and muddy water
of channel country
and raw red sandhills
farther out

come August, with signal smoke, word of mouth and pedal radio the universal message would be: 'Meet you at the Isa'.

Next year, with a cracking of whips, the stockmen would muster the ranges, sandhills and swamps for their outlaw horses and scrubber bulls. Then once again the bushmen would gather, some to test their skills, others to relive the past. Meantime, in unfenced pasture that reached to the horizon, many a stockman would test his skill all day against some outlaw horse, the only spectators to witness his great wild ride a few stockmates, a herd of bawling cattle or bleating sheep, maybe a kangaroo or dingo. For many great horsemen would never become great rodeo riders.

But now, like dry stalks of brown grass caught up in the swirl of a whirly-wind, people scattered away across the red-brown land.

11

Late in the year, with the weather getting warmer, Mulga helped a drover called Brumby and his old mate Quart-Pot to work for a station owner miles away, in a countryside of red stony hills and thick mulga forest. He wanted them to clear his place of cattle. This was called scrubber running, and they decided to take twenty stock horses with them on the job. There were big old cleanskin bulls never yarded and mobs of cows and calves, about a thousand head all told. The owner offered Brumby, Quart-Pot and Mulga shares in whatever they could muster, so much a head, and told them to shoot what was left.

They were shown around the station by the owner. He pointed out the paddocks where the quiet branded cattle ran, then took them back into the hills where the scrubbers roamed. Many men before had tried to clear the scrubbers but they always left a few, which bred up again. Now they were worse than ever. There was not much grass in the hills, but cattle could exist on mulga for years so long as there was plenty of water. They made camp and decided to build a trap around the main watering place way back in the hills. Soon, with the help of station men, they had erected a rough yard around the water and a couple of much stronger small yards with a loading ramp. Not far from the gate they built a hide of bushes and rigged up a trip wire. The cattle sometimes came to drink even as the men worked, and at night more would come to drink in small mobs, the old bulls always fighting around the dam. Around here the ground was red and stony but the cattle were in good nick. Old grass, stubble and mulga kept them going, but this did not worry the men as old bony cows were bringing good prices and the bulls were fetching bigger sums.

After finishing the yards, they left the gateway open for a few days, letting the cattle come and go undisturbed. Soon they were watering in daylight again. Then the men readied their horses, and while they waited for the cattle to settle back at the dam they rode the hills and found small rock holes filled with water. For a few days they bailed out the water so the cattle would have only one waterhole to come to. As they rode through the hills they saw the workings of old opal mines. Sometimes they fossicked for a while around the mullock heaps.

They talked about the next step in getting the cattle out of the mulga scrub into the yard. They had the use of the station truck, which carried eight or ten head at a time. They reasoned that they would trap most of the cattle in the first few days. They decided that tomorrow they would start trapping the scrubbers. When they rode up to the dam beside the yards, they noticed quite a few cattle. At their approach some headed at a gallop into the thick silvery grey forest of mulga trees. Others, unafraid, just walked away, nibbling at the leaves of the mulga trees. As the three men sat around the fire that night, they could hear the cattle coming to water. They had camped behind a stony ridge away from the dam, where they would not disturb them. At daylight, two of them would ride around in a huge circle starting the cattle towards the water, while in the bough shed watching the gate would be the third man. When enough cattle were around the dam inside the yard, he would release the trip wire and close off their escape.

Before dawn a cool breeze seemed to whisper through the leaves. The men loaded food and a swag onto the truck, then Brumby drove Mulga to the concealed hide-out and took the truck back to the camp. Silent and unseen, Mulga waited for the cattle to come to water.

Brumby and Quart-Pot then rode into the scrub, circling the dam in a wide arch, not chasing the cattle, just starting them up. Eventually they would become thirsty and would head for the dam, where they would be trapped.

Meanwhile, Mulga, his swag rolled out, waterbag full, and with some old newspapers and magazines to read, settled down till the cattle came to water. A small hole in the bushes gave him a clear view of the gateway and most of the dam. As he watched, a few cows and calves came to water, about twenty in all. Soon they were joined by more cattle. When about fifty were inside,

Mulga released the trip wire and the gate came crashing down with a thud. Some of the cattle took fright, but had nowhere to gallop. Behind the dam yard another gate opened into the two smaller, stronger yards. Mulga walked out of hiding to the gate, secured it, then walked into the yard around the dam. Flicking his stockwhip so as not to make a loud noise, which would carry to the cattle in the mulga, he hunted the trapped cattle into the smaller yards. Then he headed for the trap gate. Pulling it up by a rope hooked to a pulley, he secured the trap wire, undid the pulley rope, then retreated into his hide-out and sat down to wait for more cattle to come to water.

By nine o'clock Mulga had trapped and hunted over a hundred of the wild cattle into the smaller yards, which were now full. He now let the cattle come and go to the dam, not bothering to trap more.

At midday Brumby and Quart-Pot rode up and were pleased with the first day's work. They had lunch, then began the task of trucking the cattle to bigger, safer yards at the homestead. Loading the cattle on the makeshift ramp was slow, hard work. Finally they filled the truck, and headed off, while Mulga stayed behind to trap more cattle. By evening Brumby and Quart-Pot had made six trips to the station with cows, calves and young bulls, having drafted off the bigger older bulls. About ten of these stood in the yard. After eating a meal, they again loaded up the truck, and for half the night drove cattle to the homestead. The bulls were trucked last. It was past midnight when they crawled into their swags and slept.

The next day was the same. All day they worked trapping and trucking cattle. While they did this, transport trucks took the cattle from the station to the town, to be trucked by rail to the coastal meat works. In the yards by the dam the big old scrub bulls, still separated from the rest, fought among themselves. For three days they went on working, until they had enough cattle to fill all the wagons they had ordered. Many of the smaller calves were drafted off in the station yard, later earmarked and branded and taken to run with a quiet herd in open country. Some old piker bullocks never yarded before simply gave up and died after a few days behind the dreaded stockyard rails. It seemed to the men who had captured them that they had died from a broken spirit. Cut off from their scrubby hills they lost the will to live. The men could offer no other explanation. Those big long-horned bullocks, fat and healthy a few days before being yarded, just refused to eat or drink. After that they did not bother about the few old pikers left, except to shoot them when the station wanted meat. Eventually they would die out. The men decided it was better they roamed free in the mulga scrub and provide meat when wanted, than be yarded and cut off from freedom, to die in the yards.

After the first big trappings they had skimmed the cream from the mob; now the hard work would begin. Although they still trapped some cattle, soon they had to ride the ridges searching for the smaller mobs that drank at the hidden rock holes. When they threw the smaller bulls and cows they would push short, heavy lengths of wire through their noses, run it through a ring on the end of some rope, then tie the rope to a tree. This way the cattle could be left for a few days before they were driven to the yards. The weather was now getting hot. If they had left the scrubbers tied down with straps around their hind legs they would have died in the heat; tied to a tree by the nose, they could stand on their feet and walk around, seeking shade. At first the beasts would struggle against rope and tree, but they soon realised that the harder they fought, the worse it hurt. Mulga had often observed how strong their nostrils were. Rope and wire fixed to any other part of the body would have torn the flesh away. But the nose ring would hold forever. He'd seen bulls being taught to lead for the show ring, hooked up by a nose ring behind a tractor and dragged for yards. That thin piece of gristle between the nostrils never gave way.

After a few days of being tied up, ropes were clipped to the nose rings and the scrubbers would easily be led to the roadside, where the truck was waiting to be loaded. Just one tug brought them in the right direction, one man on horseback in front tugging on the lead, another behind. Sometimes the riders were even able to trot or canter through the undergrowth. And then they had to manhandle the cattle onto the truck – not an easy task.

After weeks of hard riding, Brumby, Quart-Pot and Mulga, sometimes with the help from a couple of stockmen employed by the station, had cleaned most of the scrubbers from the station except for the big old scrub bulls. As well as being harder to get, the bulls were worth big money. 'Hamburger meat' they were called. Sometimes they caught a fleeting glimpse of the old pikers as they galloped through the scrub, then came the sound of crashing timber and hoof beats as they headed away from the horseman who rode silently through the trees. Some looked fearsome, huge and sleek, their long needle-sharp curved horns a match for any man and horse. But the scrubber runners had a secret weapon up their sleeve: a tranquilising dart gun.

Now they gathered a few quiet cows into a mob and took them to the rugged mulga covered ridges, to use as coachers. Next day they tracked the coachers through the hills and usually they would find one or more of the big old scrub bulls with the mob. Unseen from the ridges, the men would dismount and load the darts with raw nicotine. A deadly mixture, as they soon found out. If they loaded too much the bull would die in seconds. Even a scratch to any of the men from the needles would have been instant death. As they loaded the darts they had to estimate the weight of the bulls. Not so easy when they were among a herd of cows, a hundred yards away. If the dart was loaded with too much the bull would die. If there was not enough nicotine the bull just turned into a charging menace. Although groggy, they would follow the men on horseback as they weaved and twisted. Maddened by the drug, they became more dangerous than anything the men had ever seen. After a few trials they soon mastered the use of the drug and could tell at a glance the weight of a bull. Loading the dart into the gun, they would mount up and silently approach the coachers and whatever bulls were with them. Then whoever carried the gun would charge flat-out for the target. Before the old bull realised what had happened the dart would be fired into its meaty rump. Within ten seconds the bull would start to stagger as the raw nicotine took over. As soon as it fell to the ground the men were upon it.

The first thing was the removal of the razor-sharp horns, sometimes five or six feet wide. The men knew they only had a few minutes to saw off the horns and make the bull less dangerous. As soon as they had finished, they pulled the dart from the beast, mounted up and rode away. Within a few minutes the bull would be on its feet, wanting to charge everything in sight. The men always tried to keep the quiet cattle between them and the bulls. This was how they gathered the old scrub bulls. When the bulls had recovered enough to walk they were headed towards one of the rough bush yards they had built. Once the bulls were yarded they would sometimes leap at the fence, trying to escape. But finally they would give up. They kept the bulls yarded until they had at least enough to fill a railway wagon. Most days, as the men mustered, they would break the bushy branches of the mulga trees and feed the bulls. It was strange to see the difference between the wild charging bulls and the wild piker bullocks. Whereas the bullocks, yarded, would fret and die in a few days, refusing to drink or eat, the bulls would come to the fence and eat the branches of mulga from the men's hands.

By now the men's bodies were criss-crossed with scratches from the bushy, spiky branches they constantly brushed aside. Sometimes their skin was torn and they suffered deep gashes in their backs and legs. Their shirts hung in tatters, but their tough stockmen's trousers were rarely torn. They would carry for life the scarred scratches from the trees, the legacy of those wild rides. Sometimes there was only the sound of the breaking branches of the mulga to tell of scrubbers up ahead. Then they would race flat-out, putting their trust in the stock horses as they hurdled fallen logs and, with just a touch of fingertips on the bridle rein or the pressure of a knee, steered a course through the thick spiky mulga trees. Reaching open ground, the men used their spurs, urging on the horses. Then, as they reached a beast, they reached down to grab the tail of the fleeing beast, giving a yank and a twist, horse and cattle in full flight. As the scrubber came crashing down, the men leapt from their horses and raced to grab, its hind legs, to wrap and tie them with stout bullstraps. Then they would catch up with the horses and continue the chase. Good stock horses would stop as the men leapt off. The spilled reins would fall to the ground and the trusty horse would stand until the men had finished with the scrubbers. Away they went once again, following the crashing sounds in the timber ahead.

One day as they sat around and watched a struggling bull tied to a tree, Mulga looked down at his one good pair of trousers and cursed the big rip between ankle and knee, complaining that his trousers were worth as much as the young scrubber tied to the tree. Suddenly he felt a pain in his leg. Pulling his trouser leg up, he was surprised to see a huge hunk of flesh missing from his calf, a piece of meat about four inches by two. Hardly any blood flowed from the deep gash. He must have hit a tree spike in the wild chase. They were too far away for any doctor to take a look at it – it was at least a hundred miles to the nearest town, and they were miles from the nearest station house and a first-aid kit. They mounted up and rode back to the camp. Brumby wanted to drive Mulga to the homestead to have the wound dressed. There was nothing to sew, as all the flesh had all gone. But Mulga refused. Brumby had bandages and some ointment as well as a packet of aspros in the tuckerbox. So Mulga heated some hot water on the fire and added plenty of salt, then bathed the wound, which made it sting. As they looked through the truck for ointment, Mulga remembered he had a bottle of aftershave lotion in his swag. He poured some onto the wound then almost jumped into the treetops as the pain took over. After bandaging the wound they sat making plans for tomorrow. They would have to gather the eight or nine scrubbers left tied to trees and load them onto the truck. If Mulga was fit enough he could drive the truck while Quart-Pot and Brumby brought in the cattle.

By lunch time next day they had loaded the last of the cattle. It was time to head back for the station yards. Quart-Pot drove the truck while Brumby took the horses back to camp. At the homestead the owner's wife dressed Mulga's leg and advised him to make the trip to town for an injection in case it became infected. But Mulga decided to head back to the mustering camp. He swore he would be right to ride next morning.

When he reached camp, he discovered Brumby had cooked the one and only meal he ever produced: stew. Whoever was first home was cook for the evening, and in the morning whoever rose first stirred the fire and provided breakfast while the other men attended to the horses. Brumby seemed able to cook only this one meal: stew, made from everything in the tuckerbox. Whenever Quart-Pot and Mulga drew near the camp at the end of the day they'd remark without fail: 'I bet I know what's for supper tonight!' Sure enough: stew. Quart-Pot could make good johnny-cakes and damper. Brumby could never cook proper damper. Whenever Quart-Pot and Mulga tried to eat the doughy mess, it would stick to their teeth.

This day, after yet another unsuccessful shot at baking damper, Brumby had tossed the result into the scrub. Later, when Quart-Pot and Mulga returned to camp, they sat around drinking tea for a while. As Brumby cooked supper, the horses fed on the dry stubble around the camp. Suddenly one old horse began acting funny, as though it was crippled. It hobbled around with something caught on its foot, getting into a panic. The men raced out to investigate what was wrong. As they drew nearer, they saw a round black object stuck to one front hoof. As Brumby stood back slightly, Quart-Pot and Mulga examined the horse. Mulga held its head and Quart-Pot lifted the leg and they saw at once what had caused the panic. A burnt, soggy damper. The old horse had stepped right in the middle of it. With much laughter, Quart-Pot and Mulga freed the luckless animal from the disastrous result of Brumby's baking.

Later, as they sat around the camp fire, Quart-Pot suggested that maybe they could patent Brumby's damper as a device for catching brumbies and scrubbers. They would make a fortune. Immediately they thought of the ways Brumby's damper could be used – they'd soon be rich if they had enough to scatter throughout the bush. Whenever a brumby or scrubber trod on the damper and their hooves stuck to the mixture they would be simple to catch. No more racing through the scrub, tossing bulls, tying them down. 'Just think,' said Quart-Pot, 'of all the cattle we could trap with this mixture you've invented, Brumby – we could retire to the Gold Coast, and then use it to trap a few bikini-clad sheilas!' – 'What a life!' Mulga laughed, but as Brumby slaved over the hot fire cooking supper, he did not reply. Soon it was time to eat, and as they nibbled at a new batch of harder, more edible damper, Brumby held out a piece and called to the old horse, now eating oats and chaff from a bucket. But it only lifted its head and whinnied. It wanted no more of Brumby's baking.

After supper they agreed that tomorrow they would seek out the quiet coachers again and gather the last of the big old scrubber bulls. Mulga bathed his leg, dressed it with the stuff provided by the station owner's wife and gave it another dose of aftershave lotion before wrapping it in a clean new bandage for the night. He felt sure he'd be right to muster next day.

Lying in their swags they heard the bellow of cattle from near and far. They had scattered all over the place. Many had been separated from their mates in the chase through the scrub: now they called to a mate that would never answer back. The three men knew their task was almost over. Brumby had already told Mulga and Quart-Pot they would be paid off in another week. Then Brumby would spend time alone, shooting out the few scrubbers that remained until at last only the wild piker bullocks were left. The work would suit him well: he had earned his name chasing and trapping brumby herds across the west. At other times he'd been employed as a dingo trapper. He knew the bush and its creatures as well as any man. After Mulga and Quart-Pot had departed, he would ride silently through the bush, cutting the tracks of those remaining scrubbers. Then, sniping from cover, mulga scrub echoing to gunfire, one by one they would fall to his bullets. In a few weeks' time this wild stony mulga country would be silent. Maybe in time the land would be restocked with quiet cattle ... and they in time would become wild. Then once again the wild scrub bulls would reign supreme in the grey-green forest of mulga trees and across the stony red hills. But for now the scrubber runners had won the day with their trap yards and dart gun. The scrubbers were no match for the men or the horses they rode.

Yet the work had taken its toll of the horses and they were all tired now. Three had been crippled in the mad dashes through the scrub, but the worst accident happened one day when Quart-Pot and Mulga were busy tying a scrubber to a tree. Their horses, reins trailing, stood close by. Suddenly a half-grown bull, disturbed by the chase, came crashing out of the scrub. Still struggling to secure the scrubber, the two men saw the bull heading straight towards them, head lowered to charge. At the last moment it changed course. Now straight in its path stood Mulga's stock horse, his favourite. The bull's razor-sharp horns ripped a hole in the horse's soft underbelly and parts of the stomach fell out. The bull vanished from sight. The two men, leaving the scrubber tied, rushed over to the horse, throwing him to the ground trying to calm him, trying to push the stomach back. It was hopeless. At this point Brumby appeared and saw at once what had happened. He took the dart gun from his saddlebag and mixed a lethal dose, then fired the dart into the horse's rump. It died in seconds. Killing him fast was the only way to end his agony. The men stood grim-faced and silent.

Mulga had removed the saddle from the horse as he was being held down. As he reached down to take the bridle from the horse's head, he gave him one last pat. He felt a heaviness upon him. Many long miles he had ridden that trusty old horse. Wild hard rides through the scrub and over stony hills. Galloping flat-out alongside stampeding cattle, staking his life on the horse as they rushed to the lead, then shouldering the cattle around out on the flat. Now the old horse was dead, killed by a half-grown scrubber bull. Mulga tried not to show his emotion but Brumby saw the tears that ran down his cheek. Even the other two seemed to find something to wipe from their eyes. It seemed strange that out here in the scrub, these men who saw life and death every day should be so affected. But to these men a horse was something special. Nothing stirred a stockman's heart more than a pretty girl or a good stock horse. The loss of a favourite stock horse was a disaster. To Mulga that old horse had been priceless, something money could not buy.

Brumby rode off to get the truck and pick up Mulga. Mulga carried his saddle to the road, where he sat waiting for the truck to arrive. Soon Brumby came and they drove back to camp. Still silent, they cooked supper. Mulga pictured the scene earlier in the day as the sharp-horned scrubber charged. Although it all happened in seconds, he clearly recalled the shape and colour of that bull. He would know it again anywhere – and he vowed to capture it.

Next day, in late afternoon, as Brumby, Mulga, Quart-Pot and a few of the station men were heading back to camp, riding across a ridge, they happened to look down and saw in the flat below two head of cattle. One was unmistakably the bull that killed Mulga's horse: it was red-and-white with two white patches on the ribs and a white streak along the neck. And those were the wide curved horns that had gored Mulga's horse to death the day before. At once they decided on a plan of action. They would throw the two beasts and leave them tied down for the night. Quart-Pot and Mulga would get the red-and-white bull. They started down the slope. Then one of the horses' hooves struck a stone. To the scrubbers below it was like a rifle shot. The next moment they were galloping flat-out. The horsemen riding down the slope swung their reins around the horses and niggled their sides with spurs. Tired as they were from a hard day's work, the stock horses responded to the riders' urging, stretching out their necks as they raced down, loose stones ringing as the steel-shod hooves struck them. The horsemen raised their wrists like war shields to ward off the mulga branches in front of them. Down on the level ground they were soon weaving a path through the scrub. Then the scrubbers were in sight, the riders' eyes fixed on the rumps of the two bulls as they narrowed the gap.

At last Mulga was only a few yards behind the red-and-white bull in the thick scrub. He could not look, but he knew Quart-Pot was just behind. His mind was on the branches that could drag a horseman down, and the dead dry limbs that could rip through a man's body as he raced on, never knowing what lay beyond the bushy branches of the tree ahead. Many good men had accidents like that, sometimes fatal: a head smashed in, or a failed leap across a fallen tree and horse and rider lying on the hard red ground.

As Mulga galloped behind the bull, he waited his chance to race abreast of it. Then, reaching out, he grabbed the shitty tail and wound it round his hand. Racing past, he gave one great yank on the tail: the scrubber, in full flight, was sent off-balance. It came crashing down and almost before it hit the ground Quart-Pot, close behind, was off his horse. He grabbed the bull's tail and pulled it up between the hind legs, then lay on its rump and pulled the tail tight. The scrubber could not regain its feet. Mulga, recalling yesterday's tragedy, rode back to Quart-Pot's horse and moved it away in case the bull somehow got free and killed another horse.

Then, pulling his horn-saw from beneath the saddle flap, he walked to where the bull lay struggling on the ground. As Quart-Pot still lay on its rump, Mulga took a bull-strap from across his shoulders and wrapped it around the bull's crossed legs. He then walked to the head and began to saw off those wicked horns. Usually only the sharp tip of the horn was cut off, but Mulga cut back those horns real short. As the bull struggled he was covered in the warm blood that squirted from the stubs. With both horns off, Quart-Pot and Mulga both sat on the bull's rump and waited for Brumby and the station men. They soon appeared, having thrown and tied down the other bull. They gathered Quart-Pot and

Mulga's horses and while Mulga and the others mounted up, Quart-Pot held down the bull. Then he raced to his horse and vaulted into the saddle as the enraged beast, even with its hind legs bound, got onto its feet and charged at the horses and men. They had expected the charge and managed to dodge it. The bull again lost balance and fell and the men rode off, leaving it where it lay. Tomorrow they would gather up both beasts. The horses, tired and thirsty, chomped at the bridle bit and quickened their step, eager to be home.

So after two months Quart-Pot and Mulga were finished. They were well paid for their work and took their cheques from Brumby before heading off to town. The whole bush seemed silent now. Only a few fresh tracks showed in the dust around the dam. The trap yards were empty. When they first came here the bush was alive with the sound of cattle that had roamed undisturbed for years. Now nothing stirred. The two men were glad to be gone; the excitement of the chase was over. As they loaded their swags and saddles they joked and laughed, looking forward to the bright lights of a two-pub town and their first days of leisure.

After Brumby had completed his task another saga of the West would be completed, written in blood. First the Aborigines were cleared from the land so that the cloven-hooved alien stock could graze. Then the stock became unmanageable, and now Aboriginal stockmen were used to clear the land of unwanted cattle. When would it ever end, Mulga and Quart-Pot wondered as they talked. They often discussed the true history of the land and Mulga would quote bush poets of the past, sometimes lines of his own …

Red-brown land Australia
Ancient kingdom of my grandma's clan
Your pastures sown with greed
Hillsides stained in blood
Country is my learning
I worship 'neath a mulga tree
My prayers to mother earth.

12

Mulga and some of his stockmen mates sat in the bar of an outback pub, some sipping beer, some drinking rum with beer chasers. They lit up cigarettes, mostly rolled with Log Cabin tobacco from tins whose round tops were dinted and pitted, always being used to remove the caps from beer bottles. The men were mainly dressed in their Williams riding boots, Akubra hats, stockmen-cut trousers and long-sleeved shirts with double pockets, in all colours of the rainbow. They were a mixture of types. One was short, red-faced, red-haired, his skin blotched from the fierce outback sun. Others were deeply sunburned, their skin like shrivelled leather. Some were Aboriginal, their skins varying from golden bronze to ebony black. They were the men born to the land and its climate. It was the white stockman who suffered most with his pale skin, peeling lips and skin cancers. Like their animals, white men did not adapt to the climate as Aborigines and indigenous animals had.

Inevitably their talk turned to wild cattle and horses. As they drank deeper, the horses bucked harder and the cattle became wilder. The more they drank the dimmer their minds became; some of them fantasised about things they wished had happened instead of the things that did happen. But they seemed to get on well together, these men of many colours, as they laughed and joked about misfortunes, hardships, mean bosses, terrible cooks ... After a few days in this outback town, most would be eager to get back to those hardships left behind. There was something about the solitude of the bush that beckoned these men back a hundred times. Many had sworn to give the life of a stockman away. But always, after a spell in town where everyone was governed by the clock, they returned to the bush.

The Aboriginal stockmen in this group belonged to the mob who got up years ago and helped themselves to gain equal pay and independence. They were unlike the mission Aborigines, who, when they had finished a droving or mustering job, returned to the mission and their suppression. The money they'd earned was paid into their bank accounts but they had no direct access to it. The so-called 'Protector of Aborigines' decided if these men could spend their money or not. When they needed money they went to the 'Boss fella', as they said. In some towns the local policeman was the Boss fella, he handled everything. He gave some white fellas Murris to do his work without pay – with the threat: 'Sometime send him Palm Island if he get cheeky.'

Mulga's mate, Quart-Pot, had been on a mission station when he was young, and he had told Mulga how it went when he collected or withdrew money from his bank account: 'Up to the office I'd go, sugar-bag under one arm, to get some money to buy flour, sugar, tea and bacca. Sometimes extra money for clothes. Into the office. Behind the desk 'big fella Boss' would sit, papers everywhere. Always the same questions asked: 'What you want?' – 'Money from the bank.' – 'What you want it for? You're not buying grog are you?' – 'Tucker, new boots, Boss.' 'Okay, how much you want?' – 'Twenty pound.' – 'Okay, I give you the money. First you gotta sign-em name on this paper. – What, you can't write your name? Okay, you make a cross just here.'

'I make-em mark, gives it back to the Boss. He been looking at the cross a long time, he been scratching his head. Then he says: 'This one cross no good, look – you been spell-em name wrong, see?' He waves the paper around. Then he been crush-em paper up in his hand and throw it into the wastepaper basket near his desk. He pulls out another form. 'This time you sign him proper, hey?' – 'Okay, Boss.' So I make another cross on the form, alla same like the first one. The Boss looks harder at it, then says, 'This time you been spell-em right, here's your twenty pounds, don't waste it on the grog.'

At this point Quart-Pot grinned. 'When I walk away outside, the Boss, he reaches for the wastepaper basket and takes out the rolled-up paper with the cross spelled wrong. He starts counting out more notes – one for me, one for you, one for me … But he doesn't see the Murri girl who works as his cleaner for no wage. She's been watching through the door from the next room and she sees everything. She tell me everything.'

Quart-Pot also told of the ways his own people used their positions to make money. On the mission he came from, at night the young girls were isolated from the others in a big dormitory, with an old woman left in charge. The dormitory was built about two feet off the ground. At night, the young men would want to be with the girls they loved. Below where the old women slept, the floorboards were loose; the young men would crawl under the floor and knock three times. Then the old woman in charge would say, 'What you fella want, bumping on floor? Girls all locked up for the night.' As she lifted the floorboards she'd say, 'You fella can't come in here, I'll call the Boss man.' Then the boy would say, 'I want to see my girl, I'll give ya ten bob.' – 'Wait there,' she'd say, walking into the dormitory and waking the girl in question. If the girl wanted to go with the boy, she would return to the old woman's bedroom, and the old one would lift the board, take the money, and then the girl would crawl through. Together the young lovers would writhe out from under the building to spend the night as they liked, out in the open, making love beneath the stars. Even under those sort of conditions imposed by the white man, the young found a way to love and laugh at their so-called superiors. And they realised that almost anything could be bought with money, even among their own race.

In those days gambling was a sort of religion out in the bush. Quart-Pot described how the mania for gambling that seemed to affect every mob of men, shearers and stockmen, drovers, construction workers, cockies, also found its way into the life of those Aboriginal stockmen from the missions, when they were out in the mustering camps.

Every year, while mustering was in full swing, the travelling hawker would arrive at the stations and if possible drive out to the mustering camps, where the men would be able to buy anything they wanted. The hawker would open up his huge van and put his wares on display. Sometimes he'd spread a big tarpaulin on the ground, and on this he'd display the trousers, saddle bags, quart pots, whips, blankets, torches, pocket-knives, hair cutting sets, needles, cotton, Western shirts and the famous R.M. Williams riding boots. It was like being in a big store. Although the stockmen had no money, they signed for the things they bought – there was no need of money in the mustering camps. The men bought up big, and that night when they settled down to games of dice or cards, instead of betting with matches and tobacco, they would get serious and start to stake a pocket-knife, a shirt, a blanket, a new hat, a torch, a pair of trousers, a stock whip … anything just to stay in the game. Some would end up with great heaps of clothes and blankets, shirts and trousers, even riding boots. Next morning, if a loser couldn't find his old pair of riding boots, he'd ride barefoot, until he made some sort of deal with whoever had won his brand new riding boots. Listening to Quart-Pot, Mulga thought this exploded the myth of sharing among Aborigines. One stockman would strive to own everything of value in the mustering camp.

These days, the old ways of gambling were disappearing, from the bush towns at least. Men still gambled, but there were no more S.P. Bookies. Now the government took the commission. Life was certainly changing in the outback, the drinking stockmen agreed. Take the tourists. There was an ever increasing number of them around, with cameras dangling from their necks, asking silly questions. To bushmen like Mulga and his mates, the local Australian tourists seemed as ignorant of the outback as those from overseas. Seeing Aboriginal stockmen dressed in riding gear instead of a loin cloth, and speaking English, they would always ask if there were any 'wild Aborigines' around.

And today, as Mulga and his mates sat in the bar, an American tourist bus arrived, and as usual the question was asked: 'Where are the wild Aborigines?' This prompted one old Murri to say in plain English: 'If you want to see wild blacks then I can tell you where to find some. I'll take you to them for a carton of beer and a flagon of plonk, and you can take their photo.' – 'Okay,' replied the Yank tourist and his plump powdered wife. The old Murri made the tourist pay for the carton and plonk, then said, 'Now follow me.' So out the back of the pub they strode, the old Murri in the lead, as far as the derelict stable. There, sitting around a bottle of wine, were two old Murris and two white men. 'These aren't wild blacks,' the female tourist said. 'Yes, they are,' said the Murri. 'Get your camera ready and I'll get your husband to grab the bottle of wine and pour it out. If you haven't seen wild blacks before, then you'll see them when your husband finishes pouring out the wine.' He then turned away, leaving the tourists staring at the men around the bottle of wine. When the story was told, the men laughed and the tourists took their photos of laughing Aborigines after giving them the grog. The tourists departed much wiser.

As Mulga sat in the bar watching this episode unfold, he was reminded of another case of someone seeking out wild blacks, years ago. 'I'd like to meet again a boy I once helped to capture years ago, on a big red sandhill,' he said – and the others turned to listen as he began his story.

He told them that he grew up on the fringe or yumba of one of the Western towns. All the Murris lived here. They supplied most of the workforce for the stations, the women to clean and scrub floors, mind the kids and wait on the bosses' wives. The men did mustering and fencing in those days of segregation, when racism was rife in such towns. But the Murris of this town were very independent. Most called no man master, and most could fight, so they never walked on the opposite side of the street to anyone. As kids, the Murris maintained their own form of segregation. The big red hop bush sandhill that stretched from the edge of town past the yumba for miles was the playground of the Murri kids. After a day spent in the white man's school they ran wild on that hill, the boys wearing only a pair of old ragged shorts, their shirts kept for school. Barefoot they roamed the hill, catching rabbits, shooting birds with shanghais. They ate the wild oranges called bumbles and mistletoe from the wilga tree. Sometimes there'd be a straying herd of dairy cows, and seeking out the real quiet ones they'd bail them up and milk them when they were thirsty. After rain they would track the porcupine to hollow logs or a burrow. The hill was their unfenced playground, their own piece of paradise. Cowboys and Indians was their great game: they saw a cowboy picture show every Saturday night.

Sometimes the white kids would intrude on the hill and then there would be the big shanghai fights. And unlike the Indians in the movies, who always lost, the Murri kids always seemed to hold that big red hop bush hill. Mulga smiled as he remembered the day he and five other kids watched from cover as a bunch of white kids headed for the hill. In front was a strange white kid they'd never seen before, fat, round and shiny. He walked well ahead of the rest, calling to the others who seemed reluctant to follow. They knew they could run into the Murri kids at any time. At last they reached the hill, where the hop bushes grew everywhere. The Murris hid behind them and the fat white kid strode straight into an ambush. The Murri kids emerged from cover and stood with bow and arrows, silently staring into the face of the white kid. The other town kids turned and fled, but the leader just stood there dumbfounded. Then the silence was shattered as he shrieked: 'My God, wild blacks!' And he too turned and fled, but on the heavy loose sand he was laborious and slow. Mulga raced after him, dived and brought him crashing to the sand with a perfect football tackle. The big fat kid, twice the size of any of the Murri kids that had now all gathered around him, struggled to his knees. His mates were out upon the open plain: they stopped and looked back for a moment then headed home, leaving the new kid to his own fate. The Murris gathered round and began to chant and stamp their bare feet in the sand. The white kid, hands clasped, began to pray: 'Please, God, save me from these unholy pagan blacks!'

As the Murri kids heard his prayer they began to chant louder, and the fat kid prayed louder. Until at last, at a signal from Mulga, who was the leader of the band, they stopped dancing and singing. Then a powwow: what shall we do with him, tie him up and take him prisoner? Mulga had a brainwave. He said, 'No, he's fat, we'll eat him.' The fat kid prayed louder. The Murri kids then gathered dry hop bush and very soon it was well alight. As the flames leapt higher that white kid became a blubbering fool. Then another little Murri kid said, 'Hey, you fellas, we can't eat him. No salt – you can't eat white fella without salt.' And so they agreed to let the fat kid go, telling him this was their hunting ground, taboo to the white kids. The white kid took off through the hop bush over the sand and the last they saw of him was out upon the open black soil plain, heading for the safety of the town.

Mulga told his appreciative audience that he had often wondered what became of that fat kid. He was sure that he'd always remember the day he dared to set foot upon the big red hill the Murri kids claimed their own. If only he could meet the kid now, he'd shout him to dinner. The kid was a city boy; it was his first trip to the bush. Like so many others, he stereotyped the Aborigines. Well, fifty years ago those Murri kids had staged a land rights battle. They thought they owned that big red hop bush sandhill. But come Monday morning, those wild pagan blacks were back in school studying the white man's book, while Australia and the world ignored their thousands of years of Aboriginal culture and history.

Now, sitting in the bar, Mulga thought of the incident they'd witnessed today. The one he'd just described to his mates had happened almost fifty years ago. How little things have changed, he thought. A fat white kid, fifty years ago, had mistaken him for a 'wild pagan black'. Today tourists still came looking for 'wild blacks', ignorant of the real issues.

Now the talk returned to the favourite topic of bucking horses. On every station, as they all knew, there'd be some horse that could buck and twist like a snake – and always some horseman wanting to prove himself. Sometimes the stockmen would draw for the honour of riding an outlaw horse – and the privilege of being thrown. All the men present in the bar today knew that men who boasted of never being thrown had never ridden a bucking horse in their lives. And they had all observed that the only time most men were injured was when they were with quiet horses that might suddenly kick out. They were extra careful with outlaw horses and were seldom hurt.

Mulga recalled one taffy horse on a station where he'd worked. Over the years, Taffy had thrown every man who'd ever worked there. He seemed quiet and was easy to catch and was always in the yard each day as the men caught and saddled their stock horses. 'What's this bloody useless old taffy horse doing in the yard all the time?' one of the stockmen asked. 'He's fat as a barrel – what's wrong with him?' – 'It's like this, Jack,' the others told him. 'He's pretty snaky. He's thrown every man that ever tried to ride him. He won't buck in the yard when you ride him fresh, but out in the paddock he'll wait his chance. The minute you relax you're gone.' – 'Well,' said Jack, feeling this was a real challenge, 'I'll give him a day's work.'

So Jack saddled the taffy horse and he walked away like a kids' pony. All morning they mustered stock and at dinner camp Jack was happy; still the old horse had done nothing. They mustered again, and now it was getting late. The old horse seemed tired as he walked behind the herd. Jack booted him to keep him going, then pulling out his tobacco tin he began to roll a smoke. As he snapped shut the lid of the tobacco tin, old Taffy came alive. That old horse gave an almighty buck in the air. Hit the ground and sucked back his belly, almost dragging on the ground. Jack was off-balance as Taffy rose like a rocket ship in the air and twisted, kicking out. Jack went sideways off him into a patch of bindi-eyes. The old horse stopped bucking and stood still. He'd claimed another victim. His record was intact, he had still never been ridden. As Jack pulled the bindi-eyes from his body and clothes, Mulga and another stockman had sat on their horses and laughed loudly. Mulga reminded Jack that at least he now owned a selection, for stockmen always said that when they were thrown they could always claim an area of six feet either side of where they fell. It was said some stockmen could have laid claims to a million acres in the outback if they'd pegged their claims to the ground every time they'd been thrown.

Soon Jack was back on the old horse, kicking him in the ribs and slapping him with the reins, trying to make him buck. But old Taffy just cantered off like a kids' pony again. Jack could have ridden him to hell and back from now on. But the old horse's reputation was intact. He'd thrown Jack, so the old horse was given the best; and still, every morning, he'd be in the yard.

A few weeks later, Mulga, always eyeing the horse, knew that it was time to stake his reputation on the line, like Jack. One morning, as the men saddled up, Mulga said, 'I'll work the old Taffy today.' He was soon saddled and away they went mustering, Taffy quiet as a lamb. Mulga always used spurs on the buck-jumper ones.

Just before dinner, as Mulga chased cattle, the horse must have felt him relax for a moment, because he dropped his head and bucked high. Mulga, off-balance for an instant, managed to regain his seat and began to spur Taffy, who eventually stopped bucking. He had lost his first attempt to throw Mulga.

Later that evening, as the men mustered, the old horse made two more attempts to throw him, the last only half a mile from the homestead. He failed. Old Taffy had been beaten for the first time. As the men rode up to the saddle shed to let their horses go, Mulga began to pat and rub the old horse, telling him he'd finally lost his reputation. As he unsaddled him, the old horse stood tired and dejected looking. Mulga felt a sudden sympathy for him, and on a rash impulse he threw the bridle reins over Taffy's head. Before the old horse realised what was happening, Mulga vaulted aboard him bareback.

Taffy gave a startled snort, went into the air and began to buck straight for the shed, then spun away in mid-air. Mulga, with only a handful of mane and his spurs to hang on with, was almost thrown. Then Taffy chopped back again, and Mulga regained his seat. He knew old Taffy was beaten as he went bucking straight ahead, bolting down the horse paddock with Mulga hanging on grimly. Finally, letting go his grip on the mane and using both hands, he brought Taffy to a standstill, dismounted and set him free.

Twice in one day old Taffy had lost out. He had finally been ridden. The bareback ride was icing on the cake for

Mulga. Next morning, as the horses were drafted and caught, Taffy, for the first time, was missing. Perhaps he sensed it was no longer worthwhile galloping to the yard each morning. His reputation was lost, he could never regain it. Mulga had given him two chances in one day. Later, the boss told the men that Taffy would be turned out in the big spelling paddock to live out his days in peace. No more galloping to the horse yard and waiting until another rider came along to challenge him. He was the one buck-jumping horse Mulga remembered really well from his wandering past.

So the talk went on, tossed back and forth from one man to another through the haze of cigarette smoke as the empty bottles lined up. It was just another day that Mulga spent yarning with his mates in an outback pub.

13

The years had passed quickly for Sandy, now the owner of two stations, Red Hills and Seven Mile, which he had made his home. Seven Mile had improved vastly since he bought it. The herds that roamed here were quality cattle, they always brought top prices at the sale yards and Sandy's horses were well known throughout the West. Comet, now an old horse, still roamed on Red Hills where Bindi was employed as boundary rider. All the work was now done from the head station. By now Sandy was a wealthy man and lately he had started to take things easier, although he still worked in the mustering camp and mended fences. Mary helped with the bookkeeping. The big old fallen-down homestead they had moved into years before was now renovated and restored, the other building freshly painted. The place was a show-piece.

Sandy had everything, it seemed – yet he would always look towards the distant hills and mulga forests of Mulga Downs. He wanted to own the big cattle empire where he, Bindi and Mulga had duffed the cleanskin cattle that gave him his start. Although cleanskins still roamed close by on Mulga Downs, Sandy had no need now to build up his herd. He had all the cattle he could graze on his stations. Some evenings, as he sat and sipped his whisky on the big wide verandah, there was still that dream of yesterday, to own all he could survey. And Mulga Downs was part of that. Maybe, he thought, it will all be mine someday, a cattle empire indeed. By now Sugar-Bag had retired, his position taken over by someone equally inept. Mulga Downs continued to deteriorate and the cattle herd became even more run-out, but with cattle prices high you could make profits with cattle of any description. Yes, Sandy would welcome his chance to bid for Mulga Downs.

But for now his thoughts turned to his two children away at school on the coast, young Sandy at agricultural college. Might as well give him some book learning, Sandy had decided. It was something he himself never had and not much missed. He reasoned that no matter how much book learning you had, it was wasted without practical experience and commonsense. But at least young Sandy had completed his bookkeeping course and could help with the books when he returned home.

Sandy now drove the latest model car when he went to town. His hat brim, once turned up as he raced through the scrub, was now turned down. His stockman's outfit was replaced by tweeds and polished shoes when he visited town. He had grown stouter over the years. He often thought of Mulga and of Bindi, who still worked for him at Red Hills. Sometimes he heard news of Mulga from drovers passing through. As often as not he would be miles away, still on his wandering quest. At other times, when Mulga was in the district, he would call and ask for work – there was always a job for him. He'd been offered a permanent job as head stockman but had turned it down. Not for him resting in one place, he told Sandy; he wanted to be free to come and go where he pleased, in the city or the bush. Sandy decided he was like the red dust that would never settle in one place for long.

Sandy remembered their nights camped out, when they talked of every subject. It was always Mulga who asked unanswered questions and went on searching for answers. Maybe, he thought, Mulga would find his answers one day and settle down, unlike Bindi, who would never wander far from his tribal land. His roots were planted deep within the soil. As Sandy thought of Bindi, he wondered what would happen in the future. Already land rights claims were being granted to the true guardians of the land, the tribal elders. Within a few years the pastoral lease on Red Hills would expire. Would it be renewed as a pastoral lease, he wondered. He was pretty sure Bindi would lodge a claim to the country as part of his tribal lands. Sandy was sure that both Mulga and Bindi knew about the lease on Red Hills and would have talked about it between themselves. Mulga could act like a real bush lawyer when he wanted to. Secretly, Sandy was pleased to think the land would probably be handed back to the traditional owners. He was sure Bindi would have a valid case to support his claim. It was like some silent understanding between them that Bindi should one day own part of his heritage, a piece of his Dreamtime land.

Sandy realised that Aboriginal rights had come a long way in recent years. He realised, too, how far he had come in the same time with the help of his two Murri friends. It made him think more deeply about what he really wanted. He had a wife and children, two stations, plenty of money ... It was then he realised that above all he wanted to own Mulga Downs. Then he would be truly satisfied. Just as Bindi would be contented to be granted part of his heritage. As for Mulga, Sandy knew that neither the boundary fence of his cattle empire nor the extent of Bindi's tribal empire would be big enough for him. Mulga's boundary would not end even at the state border. It went far beyond ... his interests covered the whole world.

At this point Sandy's thoughts strayed to Anne, Mary's cousin, who had come from the city to help Mary when she brought home their daughter. Anne was now married to the head stockman on Seven Mile station and had two small kids of her own. When she first arrived, Sandy noticed that she had taken to Mulga; he'd hoped she might be the one to stop his wandering way of life and make him settle down. Mulga had stayed around for a few years, then one morning he'd told Sandy he was off to somewhere or other – and that was the last Sandy saw of him for a couple of years. When he returned, he stayed only a short while. Sandy often wondered what happened between Anne and Mulga – he'd been sure they would marry. But now she was married to another.

Mary herself seemed happy here, helping with the books and running things around the house. They hired a cowboy to work around the house. Sometimes old Ten-Eighty or Dasher were employed as cowboys to help Mary with the garden and the chooks until their skin cracked, then they would head for town. Mary was boss around the house, and got on well with the workers. Her main concerns were her fruit trees and flower garden – her pride and joy, like an oasis in the desert. Sandy had never discussed with Mary the thought of buying and owning Mulga Downs. She'd been happy at Red Hills and seemed happier when they bought this place here, where they had reared their kids before they went off to school. He had many fond memories of this place, fonder ones still of Red Hills, where it all began; with himself, Bindi and Mulga, then Mary and the kids.

On the table by his chair was a letter from some graziers. They wanted Sandy to stand for the local council elections. He grinned as he read the letter. They wanted an honest, upright, hardworking man to speak for them. At least they got something right, he mused, he was hardworking. He poured himself another drink. So much had happened over the years. They had gone so fast; from the big old tin shed on Red Hills ... those were the hardest but the most carefree days. Soon young Sandy would be finished college and one day he would take over. But still Sandy felt the desire to own Mulga Downs.

Now, as he studied the graziers' letter, he wondered if he should stand for election. At least then he might get the dirt road to his stations graded more often, if nothing else. Over the years he had not been too interested in politics, but now, with a degree of wealth, came change. He was no longer the battling young poddy-dodging cocky struggling to survive and make ends meet and improve his herd. With expansion and wealth came a stronger desire to hold onto and increase his acres, and with that came the inevitable desire for power. Once, like Mulga and Bindi, Sandy had been a Labor supporter; now he supported the Country Party. When he visited town these days, he drank in the carpeted lounge of the hotel bar, attended meetings of a dozen local committees and donated to all the worthwhile charities. He got on well with stockmen and station owners alike. He had a reputation for feeding and paying his stockmen better than at most other stations. He would never be the real toff or abuse his newfound status in life. He was still called 'Sandy' by everyone, unlike others of his ilk who liked to be called 'Mr', even those who only managed stations. Such was the social structure of the bush.

Always, when driving to town, Sandy would pull up and ask drovers along the road how things were, if he could get them something from town. He'd talk a while about the country, where the good grass and water were. Yet when droving mobs passed through his land, he always made sure the mobs did not stray from the stock routes and eat too much of his grass – after all, as he'd once told Mulga, they were not the drover's cattle. They might belong to some big absentee landlord living abroad. Remembering his own early droving days, he always sent one of his stockmen to see the drovers through his boundary gate and make sure they gathered none of his cleanskins, or a bullock for a killer at the journey's end. Yet when drovers wanted to spell horses on his place he would let them use his paddocks. Not many drovers owned stations. Most ran their horses on Crown Land stock routes and had to pay heavily for the privilege of doing so when droving was over for the year.

As Sandy sat on the verandah Mary appeared and told him the cook wanted some meat. They would have to kill tonight. The stockmen were camped out, branding, which left only him and Ten-Eighty around the house to find a killer. So Sandy gathered knives from the meat-house and found the cowboy. Soon they headed out for the meat in the truck, a rifle held in place by two pieces of hoop-iron bolted above the dashboard. When Sandy went for a killer, he always drove towards the Mulga Downs boundary. Today, as they searched for a killer, a dozen times Ten-Eighty pointed out cattle that would be good to eat, but always Sandy drove past them saying, 'We'll find a better one soon.'

For an hour they searched. Ten-Eighty, who was getting annoyed, said: 'Bloody long time to find a killer.' At last Sandy pulled up at a place where about ten head of cattle stood in the mob. He reached for the rifle, took aim and fired. 'Missed the bastard!' he yelled. A fat old cow fell to the ground. – 'No, you got one,' said Ten-Eighty as they drove up to the fallen beast. Taking a knife, Sandy cut the spinal cord behind the head, then, cutting a strip from the brisket, plunged the sharp blade in deep. The hot blood came gushing out.

As they waited for the beast to bleed, Ten-Eighty, standing near the rump, noticed the brand. Never real bright, he shouted: 'Hey, this is a bloody Mulga Downs cow!'

'Yes,' said Sandy, 'I told you I missed the one I aimed at. This one was standing behind it. We may as well eat it now, no good wasting good meat.' And as they began to skin and bone the beef from the carcass of the neighbour's cow, Sandy recalled how he, Mulga and Bindi had once discussed the habit of a lot of station owners of eating only the neighbour's beef. They'd even heard tales of men being sacked because, sent out to kill, they had shot the station cattle instead of the neighbour's. That day Mulga had told Bindi the only reason Sandy never shot his own cattle for meat was because he was so fond of them. They were all pets, and he just couldn't eat his pets. Besides, other people's cattle always tasted better. Now, as they butchered the neighbour's beef this day, Sandy made up his mind to stand for council election, while Ten-Eighty deplored his ability with a gun, aiming at one beast and hitting another. Bloody useless bosses, thought Ten-Eighty, can't do anything right, should have done the shooting myself.

★

181

Talking to the stock and station agents handling the sale of Mulga Downs and adding up his assets, Sandy realised that to buy Mulga Downs he would have to sell off Seven Mile station. It would be difficult to sell Red Hills at its real value since the lease on the station was almost up. But with the sale of Seven Mile he would have enough to achieve his dream.

Unlike Mary, who loved the Seven Mile homestead, Sandy would have no qualms about leaving here and moving to Mulga Downs. The only thing he regretted in connection with Seven Mile station was that he'd never been able to discover how it got its name. He knew it must be seven miles from somewhere – but *where?*

Once they moved to Mulga Downs, Sandy realised, he would have completed a full circle in his life. In future, it would be he himself who would have to protect the vast, unfenced pastures and the unbranded herds that roamed on Mulga Downs from the poddy-dodgers – including Bindi and his mob.

Within a month he found a buyer for Seven Mile. Mary was at first very reluctant to leave the house and garden she had come to love, to return to Mulga Downs as mistress of the big house – where all those years ago, when she first came to the bush, she had served and waited on old Sugar-Bag and his jackaroos, the 'marsupials' as they were called back in those days. Gradually, however, she accepted the move. For Mary, too, the wheel had come full-circle.

★

While Bindi fought for the return of part of his tribal lands just beyond Sandy's northern boundary fence, far away in the city Mulga tinkered with the keys of an old typewriter and tried to imagine what he would write about ... He was the only one of the three friends not completely changed by circumstances, except for his greying hair and the inevitable advance of age. Sometimes he lived in the city, sometimes in the bush. In the days when the three of them used to argue about everything that came to mind, or after they'd witnessed some funny episode in town or in the bush, Mulga would often say: 'One day I'll write a story about you and all the things that happen.' But none of them had taken much notice of him. For no-one had ever seen Mulga with a pen or writing paper in his hand. They had never seen him either write or receive a letter. Always, when relaxing, he would have a book or perhaps a month-old newspaper in his hands.

However, on a recent visit to the bush, he had come to stay overnight at Seven Mile. Sitting in the station office talking to Sandy, he noted the latest computer equipment, installed with much urging from young Sandy. Then he spied a couple of old typewriters gathering dust on top of a filing cabinet. 'You've no need for those now,' he told Sandy. 'Can I have one of them? I really might try to write something, now I have the time.' So Sandy had given him one of the battered, dust-covered machines. Maybe, he thought, Mulga would write something at last, after all those years of threatening to do so ...

14

Bindi sat on the verandah at Red Hills and looked out over the mulga-covered land stretching to the horizon. He knew every inch of the country in all directions for miles around. But for him the only ground that held real meaning was that part of Red Hills and Blackwater, which was the country of his Dreamtime learning. Although he lived and worked in a white man's world, Bindi retained his tribal ties with the land. Here he was happy, helping to preserve his Aboriginal culture while planning for the future. No more, he thought, the smoky camp fires and gunyahs made from bark and branches. Things had changed now. Soon the lease on Red Hills would be finished, and then Bindi intended to lodge a claim to help ensure that his people's culture would never die out, when they were once more guardians of the land.

Good housing, proper health care and some education in the white man's world had enriched Bindi's life. But he saw the need for his children to be educated in tribal ways as well as the technology of the space age. At the same time, he understood that living in isolation would achieve nothing, only hasten the demise of his culture – cut off from the present, living in the past. Stone-age medicine would not cure the twentieth-century sickness of his people. Solutions lay in planning for the future.

Bindi wanted to keep alive his culture while enjoying the ease of modern living: the flick of a switch for light, running water, fast cars, jet planes ... Even the day of the horse was now coming to an end in the outback, with motorbikes and helicopters beginning to take over the work of the stockman's horse. He realised that his race, growing fewer all the time, could only survive and preserve their culture by becoming part of this modern world. Once they achieved this they would become strong as one tribe. No matter if one of them became a lawyer or a doctor in mainstream society, he or she would always be Aboriginal first, their bonds with the earth strong and enduring.

Without education, health and housing improvements, Bindi thought, in two hundred years' time the same old problems would exist – and the white man would be happy to let things go on like this, with his tribal brothers a tourist attraction, thrown a few coins amidst their appalling living conditions. Some, in search of knowledge, might head for the town or city, stepping out of the stone-age into the space age, but they would soon become disillusioned, unable to cope. Kept too long in ignorance, they would drink, sleep and die in parks and river beds, shunned by both black and white, unable to survive in either world. In town, Bindi often saw others of his tribal clan, dirty and drunk outside the hotel, living in squalid humpies on the fringe, with sick and dying kids. They were uneducated in either black or white culture, unable to help themselves. Doomed from birth, not only because they had forsaken their own culture, but because they had no idea where they were going. This trend would continue as long as the elders failed to recognise the present as well as the past. The past could not be changed, but the future could be shaped by the people.

For years they had fought against segregation until that battle was won. But now his brothers themselves wanted segregation, wanted all the benefits of modern technology, yet were unwilling to contribute to the present or plan for the future.

Bindi thought with dismay of the disunity among the Aborigines themselves. Mulga had once told him that before the white man came, Australia was ruled by six hundred different feuding tribal groups representing about 500,000 Aborigines. Today, only some 200,000 Aborigines existed, but sometimes it seemed there were now about six thousand warring factions. The problem of unity could only be fixed by pulling their heads out of the sand and acknowledging the present and the future as well as the past. And this would only happen when Murris sat down and talked with all classes of society, not just among themselves.

Bindi and Mulga had so often discussed and argued about these things together. To both of them it seemed the problems could only be solved by the Murris themselves; the whites had no intention of doing it for them. The Aborigines were a small minority, aliens in their own homeland, speaking through a hundred uncoordinated voices, which confused the issue more. They also realised that there were more ignorant and illiterate whites than all the blacks together. They, too, needed to be educated. In the past no-one tribal group could speak for another, and their problems differed from area to area. But with education and a new awareness of their roots, they could become united. Then maybe other people would hear and listen to the black voices in a white wilderness. Their culture would grow strong, their affinity with the land renewed.

All this was why Bindi had stressed that his children should have knowledge of both worlds. He had educated them in the culture of the past; now they would learn of the present and take heed for the future. Bindi and Nhula had four children. Their firstborn, a daughter, was away at college. Soon his eldest son would finish school. He had talked of becoming a house painter or apprentice mechanic, but no matter what he decided, first of all he would be Aboriginal and his ties with the land would endure forever. Even if he lived and worked in the city he would always be aware of his own culture.

Now, as Bindi sat on the verandah drinking strong black tea from an enamel mug, he heard Nhula talking on the telephone installed by Sandy years before, when he and Mary lived here. Nhula's mob came from farther north, from a mission-run station and township. Quite often the family would visit her country. Sometimes Bindi would recall the expedition he and Mulga had made, years ago, to rescue Comet from Forklift's place; it was then he had first told Mulga how he had gone north in search of a wife who was 'the right meat'.

By the windmill stood a mob of horses, mostly mares and foals. He watched as the foals played around the mares drinking at the trough. Whinneying and snorting, hunting the mares back into the mob, was a chestnut quarter-horse stallion. He had been introduced to put new bloodlines into the herd. Comet, the foundation sire of the great stock horses bred at Red Hills, was dead, but every now and then you could still see his mark left upon the herd in a colt or filly … a white star, the deep red bay colour: Comet's legacy was plain to see.

Mulga, back in the bush for a spell, had recently been hired by Sandy before the cattle mustering began, to help Bindi muster and brand the Red Hills horses and to break in some of the three and four-year-olds and handle the younger ones, teaching them to lead and quietening them down. Now, as Bindi watched the horses around the windmill, Mulga walked over from the shed, where years before he, Sandy and Bindi had all camped and eaten before the house was built. Although Mulga had been offered a room in the house, he still preferred the old shed, now used as a garage and workshop. A cool room had been installed: no more did meat hang for weeks in the old gauze-covered meathouse. Meat, bread and fruit kept for weeks and there was ice-cold water at the turn of a tap. Things had certainly changed.

At weekends, when the two younger kids returned from school in town, where they boarded with relatives, Mulga would often lie on the bare boards of the big verandah and talk to Bindi, Nhula and the children. Bindi would tell them tales of the starry sky above. How a lover fleeing from tribal justice flew up there forever ... and as he told the tale, a satellite would appear, a faint light seeming to weave its way among the stars. The kids would ask about the scientists who were exploring the mysteries of the universe. What the kids thought, Mulga could not imagine; he himself accepted both scientific fact and the legends of the stars.

Mulga helped to instil in the children's minds the importance of education in the struggle of their race, telling them that people all over the world, as well as animals, birds and plants, had to learn to adapt to ever-changing conditions. Otherwise, like the dinosaur, human beings would become extinct. People did not rule the world, the world ruled them; either they adapted or they died out. Maybe the Aborigines were the only race who realised that the earth itself was the most sacred thing of all; all life came from earth, all returned to it. Yet Mulga also believed that one day, man would settle among the stars. Astronauts had walked upon the moon; perhaps in the future people would be able to live there. To Mulga, this was truly the age of enlightenment. For the first time people were able to speak out, to question ingrained views and beliefs. And all this was made possible by education. There had been great changes in his own lifetime; there would be even greater changes in the next generations.

Next morning, after Nhula had cooked breakfast, Bindi yarded the few working horses and as the sun rose he and Mulga saddled up. Mulga was riding an old grey horse he'd broken in a few years before. They headed out to muster the horse herd, riding through the mulga scrub. Grass grew green and high in the flats alongside the ridges. Winter was coming in, the days getting cooler, the nights growing cold. Following the road, they saw cattle, fat and shiny as they grazed, and here and there kangaroos. Along the cattle pads were dingo tracks. For it was their yearly mating season; at night from the verandah they had listened to them howling. One would call from miles away, to be answered by a dozen more.

Soon they came upon fresh horse tracks, which led to a windmill, from where the pads snaked out from the water in all directions. While Mulga held the herd, Bindi scouted around in a circle, cutting the fresh tracks, and sending the horses he found galloping towards the water. Next they headed for a rock hole where they knew horses came to water. Bindi was in the lead. Soon he stopped and pointed out more galloping tracks and fresh manure.

Mulga took off by himself after the galloping horses. He tracked them for over a mile, then as he emerged from the scrub he saw them ahead, out on a long wide grassy flat. Their sides were white with foam from the gallop, their tails swishing as they hunted away the flies that gathered around their eyes and nostrils. As Mulga rode out of the scrub the horses spied him. Manes and tails streaming in the breeze, they bolted across the plain and Mulga urged his grey horse faster through the stirrup-high grass.

Off to his left he saw half a dozen emus racing parallel to him. By now the horses were halfway across the plain, and Mulga began to urge his horse faster, standing in the stirrup irons and leaning along the horse's neck, yelling to turn the racing horses down the grassy plain. Suddenly, from beneath his galloping horse up flew two startled plains turkeys. One managed to swerve away from the horse's hooves; the other, trying to rise, let out a squawk. Feathers flew while Mulga cursed. The old grey horse gave a loud snort, dropped his head and rose in the air with one mighty buck. Mulga was left suspended in mid-air as his horse spun away, leaving him hurtling through space. He saw the grass coming up to meet him and instinctively relaxed, putting out his hand. As he hit the ground he rolled, breaking his fall. But he still felt a jolt as his shoulder struck hard earth. As he looked up, he saw the horse still rearing and bucking. It had all happened in an instant. Regaining his feet, Mulga moved quickly towards the old horse. It stopped bucking and stood there shivering, flanks and shoulder a lather of sweat and foam. Talking to him quietly, Mulga caught up the loose reins then soothed the trembling horse. Along the horse's shoulder was a patch of blood where he had hit the luckless turkey, lying dead in the long grass close by. Mulga picked it up and tied it to his saddle bag. Looking across the open flat, he saw a dust cloud rising at the end of the plain. The galloping horses had headed in the direction of the rock hole.

He mounted up and began to canter down the grass plain. The old horse, looking back, saw the dead body of the bird bobbing about, gave another snort and again began to buck and squeal. This time, however, Mulga was ready for him. After a couple of hard kicks with his spurred boots the horse stopped bucking and took off flat-out after the vanished herd, the turkey still bouncing from the saddle bag. Mulga let the horse gallop for almost a mile then pulled him up. He smiled to himself as he thought of the little episode. The horse, he decided, had got a bigger fright than he had. And the turkey had got the biggest fright of all.

He circled farther out, hunting up more horses. Soon he reached the rock hole, where Bindi waited at the entrance to the creek that ran up to the water. Here a fence was erected across the narrow gorge that led to the rock hole. As they closed the gate and rode to the water inside the small enclosure, the horses whinnied, snorted and raced about, biting and kicking out at each other. Pretty soon, however, they settled down and sorted themselves out into their own little mobs.

The two men made a fire and soon they were sipping strong black tea and enjoying a meal of corn beef sandwiches and pickles. As they ate, Mulga told of the buster on the plain; he'd taken up another selection, as the stockman's saying went. Then he and Bindi began to talk of old time, remembering Comet and how they recaptured him from Forklift. They had never spoken of that expedition to anyone except Sandy, and for months they had expected some sort of revenge – but it never came. Later, they learned there was good reason for this. Not long after Comet had returned to Red Hills, Forklift, up to his old trick of not paying the men he employed, had been shot. By bush telegraph they heard how a young Murri, sick of trying to get his wages after months of hard work, had taken a rifle from a car parked outside a pub and aimed the fatal shot at his ex-employer. What happened to Forklift's mate no-one ever knew. Some said he was probably dealt out rough justice in the bush, his remains now part of one of the millions of anthills that stood like sentries across the land. He was never seen again – and, like Forklift, he was never missed. Around the camp fires there was general agreement that both men deserved what they got ... But the young Murri was gaoled for life.

Taking a bite from his sandwich, Mulga said: 'Gee, this tastes just like the beef I used to eat when I was working on Mulga Downs!'

Bindi, refusing to rise to the bait, made no reply. He was watching a big old goanna that had been disturbed by the horses. It crawled nearer to them. 'If we didn't already have a turkey you would be my dinner,' Bindi told it. He got up and walked towards the goanna. As he approached, it rose up on its tail and hind legs, its long red tongue flickering like some prehistoric dragon. Then, crawling around the water's edge, it sought refuge in the jumbled rocks. Both Bindi and Mulga had often seen the smaller lizards that raced like the devil on their hind legs across the ground. Was this how man evolved, Mulga used to ask himself – first on four legs, then on two, like these prehistoric reptiles?

As they rested by the rock hole, throwing scraps of bread into the greenish waters, small dark fish began to swarm around. They were like no other fish from the rivers that flowed across this land and Bindi reasoned they must come from deep within the earth, for no floodwater reached here – the water, when it rained, drained into creeks miles away. He had also seen fish around the bubbling waters of the big artesian bore, thriving in the hot, brackish water.

On a ledge not far above them were the Dreamtime cave paintings of Bindi's people. He often came to sit here and communicate with the land. He knew the meaning and significance of those paintings. And some of the huge, jumbled boulders around the water's edge were deeply etched with symbols, shapes and signs that even Bindi could not interpret. – Either that, or he refused to say what they meant. They were a reminder of an even older culture, unrecorded in the Dreamtime legends of Bindi's ancient clan. Another mystery was the rock hole itself. It never seemed to rise or fall more than a few inches, no matter how many cattle and horses watered here.

Even in dry times, the level remained steady. Obviously it was filled by some huge underground reservoir.

Before long they started the horses back on the track to the homestead. Mulga led, the turkey still tied to his saddle bag, while Bindi hunted up the tailers at the rear, gathering a few more horses as they went.

As soon as the horses were yarded, they unsaddled, Mulga plucked the turkey and handed it to Nhula for cooking. It made a good meal.

Next morning they started early, drafting off the horses to be broken and the younger ones to be branded, the colts gelded. Soon they began the task of handling the unbranded ones, quietening them down, teaching them to lead and lift their hooves. For days they worked in the yards with the horses, handling some, mouthing others about to be broken in, until at last they had all the unbranded horses handled and quiet. Then it was an easy enough task to brand them. It wasn't long before they had all of them going outside the yard, being ridden through the bush. They were almost ready now for the cattle mustering about to begin.

Meantime, Bindi and Mulga repaired the yards and checked the fences of the cattle holding paddocks. As they drove around fixing broken wires and renewing fallen posts, they would sometimes see the rotted carcass of a kangaroo or emu twisted in the fence wire. When the roos tried to jump the fence, their legs would become caught between the two top wires. They hit the ground head-first, their legs suspended, and there they would stay, enduring a slow, painful death unless some stockman rode by and released them. Usually, however, it was only the bones and skins of the animals the stockmen saw as they rode past.

Death lurked everywhere out here. As the stockmen mustered through the scrub they often came upon the withered hide and bones of some curled and looped horned cattle. In dry times the cattle foraged in the thick mulga branches, reaching higher into the tree and sometimes standing on their hind legs to reach the juiciest leaves. Then those curled and looped horns became caught in the branches and there they stayed, hanging by the horns, only their hind legs on the ground. Months or perhaps years later some stockman riding past would see the skeleton remains still hanging from the branches. In the same way, in sheep country, the big old rams could become caught; like the cattle, they died an agonising death. Even horses were occasionally found with their heads or front legs caught, suffering the same slow agony.

The men observed that it was mostly the native animals that died in the man-made fences, while only the alien sheep, cattle and horses died caught up in native trees.

Now all the horses were broken in and shod, the yards and fences repaired. It was time for the cattle muster to start. While Mulga and Bindi toiled the days had become much colder. The stars glowed in the deep blue night; the ground below seemed to be illuminated by the gleam from a million glittering points. Winter had come.

15

It was race day at Dry Springs, and Mulga was there among the crowd. Unlike the picnic races at Mulga Downs, where registered and unregistered horses, grass or corn fed, raced together, at Dry Springs all the horses were unregistered and grass fed, straight out of the paddock. Station folk from miles around travelled to Dry Springs through the thick red mulga over dusty roads.

Mulga and Billy, one of his stockman mates, had walked twenty horses some sixty miles to get there from the station where they were working. Some of their horses were good, fast stock horses, some were bolters and there were a couple that bucked like hell. Nice, big racy looking horses they were, the ones that bolted and bucked. They would all be sold at the yards on race day. All the horses had to be auctioned, but if you had three horses you could reserve one of them. So the stations that had likely winners among their herd would put in two duds, to be bought by an unwary bidder, and reserve their best horse.

The day before the races the horses were spelled. Mulga and the other stockmen sat around and boasted about the quality horses they had brought to the meeting. They camped around the Dry Springs station and racetrack, which was really the station airstrip, set amid a forest of mulga trees. The horses raced straight down the half-mile of graded strip. Mulga watched as a couple of jackaroos stuck two posts in the ground, one on either side of the airstrip. These were the winning posts. The judge would get behind one post and line it up with the one on the opposite side. He'd have a rough idea of which horse won. Fifty yards beyond the winning posts the mulga scrub began, littered with fallen branches, while the red ground was pockmarked with rabbit burrows.

'I'd hate to be the man that buys that big chestnut horse we brought in, the one you always ride, and be on its back when it goes past the post,' remarked Billy. He'd often seen Mulga ride the big horse and knew that while it was very fast, it had no mouth. It took ages to stop after it had been going at full gallop. Mulga used him mostly for chasing horses and wild cattle – and he always said you needed a windlass to pull him up or turn him. He was one of the best looking horses in the mob, but – 'God help the poor bastard who buys him,' said Mulga, looking towards the mulga scrub and rabbit burrows.

As night fell the men put the finishing touches to the racetrack. All around the red earth was already churned into fine powdery bulldust; tomorrow, with the stomp of many booted feet it would become a dust bowl. In the darkness the camp fires glowed and the stockmen produced bottles of rum as they settled down once more to tell tall tales of horses and horsemen. The lights of Dry Springs homestead blazed forth. Social differences were plain to see: the bosses and jackaroos at the homestead, the stockmen's quarters on the outer edge, and the visiting stockmen, boundary riders, doggers and other bush workers camped in the scrub, some with their wives and kids. Yet tomorrow there would be no class distinction on the airstrip as the riders tried by fair means or foul to win.

Mulga awoke next day as the morning star arose – glinting like some huge diamond, he thought as he stoked the fire. A reddening glow suffused the cold wintry sky. Already there was movement as the racehorses began to be mustered and drafted to the sound of cracking whips and loud curses.

The auction was held in a big yard made by tying rails around the trees. Several smaller holding yards were made in a similar way. Under a rough bough shed some old doors lay across forty-four gallon drums to act as bars and food tables. The horses were now a milling, whinnying mob in the big holding yard and would-be buyers gathered at the rails to bid for the pleasure of owning a racehorse for the day, stockmen, daggers and fencers bidding against station owners and managers. The prices they bid far outweighed the value of the prizes offered – first prize for each event was some trophy valued at perhaps a fiver. But to the winners, those trophies would be cherished as if they were the Melbourne Cup.

As Mulga's chestnut horse came through the sale ring, one station manager asked him: 'Is he any good – can he gallop?' – 'My oath,' Mulga replied, 'he's one of the fastest horses I've ever rode. I keep him for chasing brumbies – even ran down a dingo on him once.'

After the horse sale was over, Billy said to Mulga: 'Ya didn't tell that poor bastard it takes two men and a boy to pull the bastard up when he's flat out, or that he bucks like hell.' – 'No,' said Mulga. 'He will win a race, though. But what happens after the race is anyone's guess.'

Now horses and people gathered at the airstrip, where among the trees the makeshift bars were open for business and the food tables were covered with a fine layer of red bulldust. A battered old ute was parked near the winning post, in the back a table, chair, waterbag and a bottle of rum. The judge and his offsiders sat on the hood or stood in the dust as the officials got the meeting underway, calling for starters to get ready for the first race.

As the horses were saddled there were many curses from the owners and riders of horses bought in the sale that bucked or bolted on the way to the start. At the end of the airstrip the starter, mounted on the station night horse, stockwhip in hand, assembled the twenty starters in some sort of line across the track, then with one loud *crack* of the whip they were off. As the field jumped away, some horses wanted to race, others jumped off the mark, dropped their heads and bucked; with the starter laughing his head off, about six of the twenty starters bucked and squealed, and soon five of the six riders were thrown in the dust. The sixth, still riding his horse, slapped it down the shoulder with his hat, gave a couple of loud *coo-ees,* and took off after the field, by now only a cloud of red dust nearing the winning post. As the loose horses were captured and returned to their owner for the day, there was much swearing among mulga trees as the owners cursed the people who'd told them they were buying good horses. Yet some of these same men, cursing how they had been duped, would be smiling secretly as they thought to themselves: 'You just wait, ya bastard, till ya saddle up the horse I put in the sale! He bucks, bites, and strikes, and if he gets into a gallop he'll fall over!'

After the first race, Mulga and a battered-faced ex-jockey named Ned (his other name was Kelly), drank a rum together. Someone said that Ned was a registered jockey warned off for life; he still sneaked around the unregistered races, and the tricks he used to win were many and dirty. He and his mate had bought horses from another station that day and were sure they would win some races. To Ned winning was everything by fair means or foul. Now he tried to enlist Mulga's aid in winning the next race, in which the jockeys rode their horses bareback. Ned had heard the Dry Springs mob brag that the horse they'd entered in this race was unbeatable. Ned, always looking for a challenge, had decided he would put a stop to that and win the race himself. But Mulga said, 'No way. Get someone else to help you,' and walked off. Mulga himself was a starter in the bareback race.

Soon the riders got ready for the race. An unregistered bookmaker operated on the course, but a limit was placed on the bets and odds given. All the bookie's winnings were supposed to go to charity. Ned placed his bet then mounted up and together with the twenty-five other horses, including Mulga, headed for the starting line. As the starter told the riders to form a line, Mulga, on one side of the track next to the Dry Springs horse (now odds-on to win) urged his horse forward. He paid no attention as Ned nudged his horse into line between Mulga and the favourite, while Ned's mate took up a place on the other side of the favourite. None of the riders had jockey-whips. They just broke a limb from a tree and stripped it of leaves. The green mulga was ideal for this. Now one thing Mulga did notice was the length of the sticks Ned and his mate carried. They seemed extra long – but that was soon forgotten as Mulga, knowing he had a fast horse under him, thought to himself, I'll give these bastards a fright. He knew Ned would try something to get the favourite beaten.

The starter's whip cracked and away they raced. Out of the corner of his eye Mulga saw a few horses jump out, then a rider flying through the air as his horse bucked. Then he settled down to ride his horse, urging him faster, keeping right up with the leaders. Suddenly he was distracted by loud swearing; glancing sideways, he saw Ned and his mate, their long whips waving in the wind. They had the favourite between them, and as they thundered down the airstrip and the jackaroo on the favourite tried to get between them they would tap the favourite on the nose with their whips. As its rider cursed and swore at Ned and his mate, Mulga, sitting sideways on his horse, watched as they opened up the gap for the favourite to come through. 'Come on, mate,' said Ned, 'we were only joking.' With a sigh of relief the unfortunate rider of the favourite urged his horse forward in a few strides. When it was almost abreast of the other two, with sticks waving wildly they again closed the gap with hard hits on the favourite's nose.

Mulga, laughing his head off, glanced around the field. He was just ahead of Ned and his mate and the other horses were nowhere. While Ned tried to stop the favourite, Mulga decided he would beat them all. He gave his old horse a couple of slaps with the swish he carried, and turned briefly to laugh at Ned, who realised for the first time that another horse was about to beat him. He began to ride out his horse like a true professional. Mulga, knowing he had Ned's mount beaten, was still laughing. With Ned cursing Mulga and the favourite's jockey still cursing Ned, they thundered towards the winning posts. Then Mulga, looking ahead, saw a bolter on the opposite side of the track get up to pip him on the post. As they reached the post Mulga, Ned, his mate and the favourite's jockey were all cursing – and then everyone was cursing as they tried to pull up their mounts before they reached the trees and rabbit burrows.

Mulga's old mount was easy to control; he pulled up and watched the others as they tried to steady their horses. As Ned began to steady his mount, Mulga saw the jackaroo on the favourite urging his horse faster, trying to catch up to Ned and his mate. Ned pulled out the whip once more, trying to keep ahead and riding straight for the mulga trees and rabbit burrows. The favourite, now flat-out, was closing on him fast – then they were all lost in the trees, and Mulga could hear the cracking of branches and loud curses as the chase went on. Meanwhile, most of the crowd remained ignorant of the drama taking place in the scrub. 'I hope that poor bastard chasing Ned and his mate doesn't catch them,' Mulga thought as he turned back. He knew that Ned fought the way he rode, to win by fair means or foul.

As Mulga rode back past the judge in the back of the ute, he told Mulga: 'If this was a registered meeting you would be sent out for life for not riding your horse out. You should never have been beaten but there you were, sitting sideways and laughing. As for old Ned, I hope that bloody jackaroo chases him back to where he came from.'

Horses and riders straggled back to the yards and eventually the jackaroo rider of the favourite turned up as well, his once clean shirt now shredded and torn from the spiky branches of the mulga trees. His mates gathered around as he told of the foul deed done by Ned and his mate during the race. It wasn't sporting, he complained. By now everyone knew what had happened, and as they drank their grog they laughed at the jackaroo's complaint.

Ned and his mate only returned when everything had cooled down. By now the whole thing had become a huge joke. Even Mulga, who should have won, and the luckless jackaroo ended up laughing about the race. Ned himself was the biggest loser, for he'd backed his own horse to win and lost his money. So in the end the joke was on him.

By now all those who had come dressed up in clean white shirts and frocks were a dusty reddish colour. One old man and his wife stood out in the crowd: he wore a morning suit, as though he was attending the races at Royal Ascot or maybe Randwick, dressed to the knocker as one old bushie said: striped trousers, coat and tails, top hat, gold cane, the lot. He was real class, Ned said as he watched the old man, who'd come out for the races invited by his son, a jackaroo on some other station nearby. Evidently he had attended posh picnic races in more settled areas before; out here he looked like a fish out of water. His greenish coloured Rolls Royce parked alongside the track was now covered in a film of fine red dust. But even he joined in the fun. Shuffling through the bulldust he came over to where Ned and Mulga sat with the horses, drinking rum from a battered and blackened old quart pot. Soon they were talking like old friends and they poured the toff a nip of rum into the quart pot. He told them of the big city racetrack – brushing away the flies he spoke of manicured lawns and flowers, the grass racecourse, the ice-cold drinks from sparkling glasses. But, he said as they refilled the quart pot, none of that could compare with this race meeting; he said it was the best time he'd ever enjoyed at the races, despite the flies, red dust, wild horses and lack of rules. Covered in dust, he strolled around happily. In years to come he would probably sit amid the flowers at some great southern racetrack and while he sipped champagne he'd tell of this outback race meeting to unbelieving friends in the members' stand.

Now the main race, the Cup, was about to begin. The riders could use any type of saddle they wished: jockey pad, stock saddle, or they could ride bareback as long as they stayed on. There were no weight conditions – the horses just carried whatever the jockey and saddle weighed. It was the same with numbers or colours – there were none, unless someone specially wanted to use them. Mulga watched a bloke who had bought his chestnut horse; he kicked it in the gut with spurs to loosen him up before the race. The horse immediately jumped in the air and began to buck among the people and the cars, crashing into the side of the Rolls Royce before the rider gained control and leaving a dent in one side – another reminder to the old toff that his visit outback was real and not a dream. He actually smiled as the horse bucked into his car, thinking, would they believe him when he told how the dent came to be there?

Ned was mounted on his best horse, confident he would win the Cup. But unknown to him Dry Springs had about eight horses in the Cup, and before mounting up the riders had all thrown away their short sticks and broken longer ones from the limbs of trees. Most of them would try to stop Ned any way they could. They began to line up, then like the Charge of the Light Brigade they were off, horses bucking, men yelling and cursing. Ned was on the extreme outside to avoid interference from bucking horses and any funny business. He rode hard for the lead, but about five Dry Springs horses were faster off the mark than him. With their riders waving their long mulga whips and cursing and screaming at Ned, they cut off his path to the line right on the edge of the graded track. Ned began to yell and call 'Foul!' as the field raced for the winning post. He was shoved right off the track onto the grass and rough going as five Dry Springs riders kept boring out on top of him, until at last he was carried away into the scrub alongside the track, taking no part in the race at all. The spectators cheered as they realised the drama taking place on the far side of the track.

The Cup was finally won by the chestnut horse Mulga had sold its rider, who was still smiling half a hour later when he finally managed to stop the horse. It was much later that Ned returned to the crowd, cursing the bloody dirty riders that rode in races around here. By then the last race had been run and Ned and his mate had not won any of them. Neither had many others, but it was a day to remember – especially for the old toff in his flash clothes and his dirty Rolls Royce.

With the sun now a dull gold fireball in the western sky, stockmen took the horses back to the holding paddocks while others still looked for missing horses gone bush after throwing their riders at the start. As the shadows lengthened the hunters returned, some with horses, others empty-handed, for the fence around the racetrack was really a big paddock ten miles long by twenty miles wide. Some horses would come back by morning, looking for water; but for the moment as the crowd gathered around the homestead to eat, drink, dance and sing, nothing really mattered.

The party that night went on until next morning. Mulga, Ned, and about ten others sat around and talked. With them was a boundary rider from a nearby station. He spent most of his time riding around on horseback looking down at the top wire of the fences, and he was nicknamed 'Top-Wire Bob'. He was living with a woman known as Bub, but not legally married to her, and they had two children who were now asleep in the tent they had erected after driving forty miles to Dry Springs in a four-wheeled sulky they owned. They were a happy couple. Both liked a drink, and they would often join in sing-songs around the fire or bush poetry recitals by stockmen.

Tonight, the topic around the camp fire turned to marriage. By now everyone was well primed, and Top-Wire Bob and Bub began to talk of their desire to become legally married. Ned, who had never been to church in his life, said they could be married straightaway; they had no need for a church wedding. And he told them about the bushman's law of 'jumping the broomstick'. It was well known, said Ned, that plenty of these marriages took place in the old days. After much talking, he convinced Top-Wire Bob, Bub and many of the now drunken bushmen and women around the fire that he could perform this simple wedding ceremony of jumping the broomstick, and at last Top-Wire Bob and Bub decided to let Ned marry them. Ned said they should have a broom handle, but seeing as there were none out here, he picked up a piece of long straight wood from near the fire, then told Top-Wire Bob and Bub that they needed six witnesses. Ned was very agile; he showed them how they had to hold the stick in both hands while jumping over it. He told Top-Wire Bob to go first, calling on the witnesses to watch as that would make it all legally binding. Top-Wire Bob was very active on his feet and easily jumped three times over the stick. He was about to have a celebration drink when Ned, now getting warmed up, said: 'Wait a moment, mate, ya gotta jump backwards over the stick as well to make it really and truly legal.' So Top-Wire Bob jumped backwards over the stick while the onlookers clapped and cheered.

Then Bub, a bit reluctant and still not real sure if this would make their marriage legal, was urged on by Top-Wire Bob and the others to take the stick, kicking off her shoes. After a couple of falls she eventually jumped three times forwards over the stick, but every time she tried to jump backwards she fell in the soft red bulldust. As she struggled to her feet, her disappointment was plain to see; in the flames from the fire her face showed despair. But all was not lost as Ned, downing another drink, told Bub that under some little known law, he, being a jockey warned off racetracks for life, could still pronounce them man and wife – but it would need more rum. So Top-Wire Bob produced two full bottles, and as they stood around the fire Ned pronounced them man and wife.

When the sun rose next morning some of them were still sitting around the fire celebrating the wedding. Word soon spread and other stockmen came up to congratulate the newly married couple. Mulga noticed that everyone now called Bub 'Missus' – nothing else, just 'Missus'.

Later in the day Top-Wire Bob, Missus and their kids hitched up their two buggy horses and started for home. Soon everyone packed up to leave. By tomorrow night all would return to normal around the Dry Springs homestead. The old toff in his dusty and dented Rolls Royce waved goodbye as he went past the horse yard and the men watched from the stockyard rail as he headed south, leaving a thick red plume of dust behind him. Ned sitting on the rail, said: 'We should have asked the old toff to the wedding last night, then he would have had a real tale for his friends in the members' stand at Randwick!'

Ned was still harping on about the crooked Dry Springs riders who forced him off the track in the Cup. He was silent, however, when asked about the bareback race when he had stopped the favourite from winning. 'Bloody cheats,' Mulga heard him mutter as he drafted his horses ready for the long, slow ride home.

16

Sandy moved to Mulga Downs after Bindi and his people won their land rights claim to Red Hills and part of Blackwater, where some of his people still lived. Bindi realised he would now have to make the station pay its way, and when his people were not employed on other stations they were asked to help with improvements on Red Hills. The station would never be big enough to support them all working for wages, so while some worked in the towns and on other stations, Bindi managed Red Hills and his people were free to come and go as they pleased. In this way there was no shortage of help whenever Bindi mustered for branding, or when he drafted the fat cattle for market. They would drove their own cattle to market, not bothering with the modern road trains for transport, which only put money in the pocket of rich transport companies. Part of the money gained from the cattle sales was paid to the young while they learned to handle stock.

Bindi realised that the pastoral industry was the only one, besides mining, that provided jobs in the inland, whether in sheep or cattle country. The only other way of making money was the untapped tourist trade, but even within their own country the Aborigines were being exploited by white tourist companies.

First their land had been taken so that alien stock could graze, then the minerals were dug from the ground to support and improve the lifestyle of the white, while the Aborigine was pushed farther and farther back into the dry, arid interior, no good for grazing. Then the tourists started to come, to see the 'natural Australia' and its untainted beauty, a part of Paradise still not lost and known for years to the original Australians. Money hungry people had discovered the tourist dollar. This once horrid dry inland, worthless for grazing, unwanted by anyone except as a place for blacks, away from the white cities, was now worth money. And still the only real beneficiary was the white man who managed the tourist trade. Even the sacred sites of the Aborigines were being exploited for the last holy dollar.

The Aborigine was urged to sit and smile as the tourist camera clicked. The tourist dollars rolled in, but not to the players who posed for the photos. They were given a pat on the head. 'Thank you, Jacky, we been gib you land back, you happy now, hey. You gottem land, you look after it. Tomorrow more tourists come, you make-em tourist bus man and resort owner rich. Money no good to you fellas out here, you catch-em kangaroo, goanna, plenty tucker.'

It seemed to Mulga and Bindi that now the only way the Murris could go was up. First their land was taken and they themselves were exploited by the pastoralists as slave labour. Then their land was left bare after mining and over-grazing and the atomic bomb tests that left a legacy of poisoned earth and sickness, still existing today. And this same poisoned land, now seen as worthless, was handed back to the Aborigines, who were told, 'Look after your land, this you home.' But many of the elders still remembered the black cloud of death that drifted over them and the sickness that was their compensation while the Geiger counters clicked over the toxic wasteland.

The Murris themselves and their culture were now being exploited for the tourist dollar because white Australian history had a very black past that one day would have to be acknowledged – for Australia's true history would be written by Aborigines, not by whites. The white Australian culture dated back two hundred years; the black culture was over a hundred thousand years old. Both could flourish together, but it was the contrast in lifestyles in this so-called democracy that worried many. While the white settlers enjoyed wealth and leisure, the Murris still lived in poverty. 'Gotta help yourself,' they were told, but at the same time they were denied jobs and education and urged to stay on tribal land, away from the towns where they might take away jobs from new white migrants and the descendants of migrants who arrived two hundred years ago.

Bindi and Mulga had seen some places where their people had isolated themselves from the real world. They were unable to cope, dying of diseases curable with modern medicines, the older people wiped out not by poisoned flour or bullets but by their own hand, with alcohol and above all because of their ignorance of the real world. In a hundred years' time everything could still be the same. Unless their lifestyle changed, who would be alive to preserve their culture?

One day Bindi, Mulga and old Quart-Pot went to a meeting held in the hotel to discuss land rights. A rich squatter whose family controlled thousands of acres boasted of his great heritage. Three generations of his family, he proclaimed, had ties to the land and the money that flowed from it. His (not so ancient) ancestors had been the first, he said, to settle the land. (After feeding some troublesome blacks poisoned flour, they had prospered ever since.) The squatter said that if the Aborigines wanted land they would have to buy it, like everyone else.

As he paused to have a nip of whisky, Quart-Pot stood up. 'How we fella gonna buy him back station land? No money, boy. We gib you fella sugar, tea, might be you take-em for station, might be we been gib you real good price, self-raising flour, no poison in him, what you reckon 'bout that, hey? We buy-em back land from you fella for self-raising flour, much better than poison flour.'

But by now the squatter was moving back to the private lounge, leaving the working men, black and white, to argue among themselves.

Mulga and Bindi often recalled the past as they drove around Red Hills Station looking at the few cattle that grazed here now. For when Bindi's mob had been granted land rights, they had to borrow money in order to start a herd. Now it was growing, but Bindi knew the station would never be able to support all his people. That was not such a worry, however. It was here he could teach the youngsters their culture and train them for jobs in the real world while they were learning modern education.

Driving around the boundary fence between Mulga Downs and Red Hills, Mulga noticed the cleanskins that still roamed the unfenced pastures now owned by Sandy, where years before they had chased and branded cattle in the time of old Sugar-Bag. Now they sat down by the stony creek where they had walked the unbranded cattle through the boundary in pouring rain, all those years ago. They talked of the past, and Mulga thought how strange it was that Sandy now owned the 'back paddock', as they called Mulga Downs, and that Bindi was guardian of Red Hills. As for himself ... he still sought answers.

As they sat in the car a big cleanskin bull walked by, taking no notice of them. Just like the old days, Mulga thought. Mulga Downs was still too big to be managed and mustered properly. Sandy's stockmen rarely mustered out here and still the cleanskins and scrubbers roamed free.

'You'd think Sandy would control his herd better – there must be enough cleanskins out there to stock a small station,' Bindi said. Then he started the car and drove back to Red Hills.

Mustering and branding was going on in the yard. Bindi's sons now did the mustering with others of his clan. Most of the work was left to the younger ones. Bindi had taught them all he knew. After the branding was over, Bindi, Mulga and the boys sat on the verandah and drank tea, talking about the next muster. One of the boys said he had seen some Red Hills cattle over the boundary fence. Why not get them back, he said. They might have to wait a year for Sandy to muster and send back the Red Hills cattle. Besides, he added, there were plenty of cleanskins over there: they could get them as well. Bindi listened to what he had to say, but in the end he told them to muster elsewhere.

Later, Bindi told Mulga that was not the first time the boys had raised the question of helping themselves to Mulga Downs cleanskins ... yet he was sure they knew nothing of the old days, when Sandy, he and Mulga had helped themselves to their neighbour's cattle. Bindi said he was aware that sometimes, mustering along the boundary, the boys would gather a cleanskin on the other side. They used a familiar argument: they said they were doing Sandy a favour by mustering his wild, unmanageable herd.

While Bindi talked, Mulga wondered – did Sandy still kill his neighbour's cattle for meat and did Bindi eat his own beef? He was sure Sandy must have noticed cleanskins missing in the hurried musters on Mulga Downs, and remembered how he had helped himself to old Sugar-Bag's cattle. He never asked those questions, but no matter on which station he had a meal, the meat always tasted good. As he looked out over the red hills and mulga forest towards the Mulga Downs homestead, he wondered what Sandy thought about Bindi as a neighbour. Would Bindi ever have the urge to expand in the future – would the next generation want more, and, like Sandy, would they turn their sights across the tree tops to Mulga Downs and dream of a cattle as well as a tribal empire?

Mulga had seen the changes wealth and power had brought to many people he knew. For him, land rights would be a four by eight plot of earth, of that he was sure. He was also sure that when man stopped thinking and improving his way of life, he would remain static, and then the only way was downward for all mankind. But maybe he himself would live to see a flight to the stars ...

Mulga returned to the present as Bindi began yelling loudly at some of his grandchildren, galloping wildly past as they chased one another. And Mulga recalled how he had sat and watched Sandy's kids do the same thing in this very spot.

On the wide, cool verandah at Mulga Downs homestead, Sandy sat sipping whisky and ice-cold water. It was a hot summer day. Relaxed by the whisky, he stared into the shimmering haze beyond the paddock fence, where the stock route ran. He remembered how he used to drive cattle and horses through the gate in the old days and recalled how he would sometimes look towards the homestead and think how good it would be to sit back on the big verandah in an easy chair, feet up on the table, sipping a cool drink and waited on by a housemaid. Then he would close the gate and head off after the stock, for those were only the dreams of a young drover.

But he recalled how often he thought how good it would be to drive his own cattle and not someone else's, how he had worked so hard on the stock route, first of all with his father. He recalled his father's pleasure at owning a piece of dirt himself, when he bought Red Hills. Then his father had died and he was left with the station and no money to stock the place. He gazed across silver mulga tree tops towards the red hills from which the station took its name, now purple in the haze. He visualised the big 'back paddock' of Mulga Downs where he, Mulga and Bindi had worked day and night duffing the cleanskins to stock Red Hills. He had never thought of this as stealing; the cattle carried no man's brand, and old Sugar-Bag and his men were incapable of mustering them. After all these years, Sandy still thought he'd done Sugar-Bag a good turn by helping to control his vast, unmanageable herd.

Suddenly he sat up in his chair. A few days before, while inspecting the station, he had seen the cleanskins that roamed the still unfenced pastures of Mulga Downs. He'd thought of Bindi, now the guardian of Red Hills, and smiled to himself as he wondered whether Bindi and his mob would help themselves to his unbranded cattle. He began to think how he could protect and hold what he had gained. He'd have to speak with his son, now overseer of Mulga Downs.

As Sandy sat and pondered on the past the housemaid bought him cake and a pot of tea on a silver tray. As he sipped his tea and gazed out across his kingdom, he thought of the droving days of soggy dampers, tea from a blackened battered billy can, sitting cross-legged around a camp fire. He realised that somehow, tea in a china cup didn't taste as good as it had in the past, drinking from a chipped enamel mug.

Distracted by some horsemen riding past after a day's work, he looked across to where only a few posts and rails still marked the old bush racetrack, where he had asked Mary to marry him after Comet's victory in the Mulga Downs Cup. He recalled how Bindi and Mulga rode across country to recapture Comet and how they had celebrated that night at Red Hills. Even Mary, who had been away at the time, never knew how Comet had returned.

Sandy thought of the good times and the bad. He had always had one secret desire, to own this cattle empire called Mulga Downs. Now, wealthy and respectable, he had found a new sort of power. He sat on the board of this and that, he was a local council member, and was being urged to stand as mayor for Muddy Gully. But he was in no hurry to decide about that.

For the moment he would concentrate on the running of Mulga Downs, culling and rebuilding the run-out herd. He'd see if his son and the men he employed could muster and clean the big unfenced area alongside Red Hills, where the cleanskins might become a temptation that Bindi and his mob could not resist. Bindi had bought the cattle brand of Red Hills after Sandy and his men had mustered and sold most of the herd – then, as a favour to his old mate, Sandy had let him buy a few hundred cows that were left. He knew they had no more money to buy other cattle. They would take ages to build up the Red Hills herd. He wondered if Bindi's mob would wait patiently, year after year, for the herd to grow. What if they did duff the cleanskins he and his men could not muster? Would he really want to know? He thought not – and yet he felt an urge to protect everything he owned, even from Bindi.

Both his son and daughter were now married and had children. His son, like him, felt tied to the land but his daughter saw it only as a place to make money, preferring the bright lights of the city. As the sunlight faded Sandy sat silent. It grew dark and the trees around the station dam became alive with screeching birds seeking sleeping room in the branches.

The homestead lights came on, and starlight was eclipsed by the glare of electricity. Sandy stirred and moved to the lounge room, walking across the carpeted floor to a padded chair where he watched television. Again he thought how things had changed: once his lounge room was the unfenced pasture of the stock routes or a mustering camp, sitting cross-legged on the ground around the fire, listening to the latest news on the old valve radio, straining to hear the headlines amid the loud static. And after listening to the news the men would lie in their swags and argue over the rights and wrongs of things, while a billion stars gleamed and glittered, pulsated and throbbed in the sky.

As Sandy watched the weather report he recalled the long wet nights when he had watched over the cattle. Sometimes a lightning flash seemed to run along the glistening horns of the restless beasts, and at a deafening thunder clap the cattle would stampede into the inky blackness. Then both night horse and rider, heedless of the wet slippery ground, raced for the lead to swing them around until they settled once more and the storm had passed, when the stock horse would continue his slow death march around the herd.

At this point Sandy shook himself and returned to the present; today he transported most of his vast herd to market by road trains. But he was pleased to have his recollections of the drover's life. His thoughts were interrupted by the ringing of the old Condamine horse-bell that signalled supper time, and as he seated himself at the head of the dining table he recalled how in the old days when he worked here, only Sugar-Bag and his jackaroos sat at the table in the big house. Sandy, with all the other workers, including Mary, sat in another room next to the kitchen. Tonight, besides Mary and himself, their son and daughter-in-law with their children and a visiting stock and station agent sat around the big old table, served by the young housemaid. Just as Mary had once waited on Sugar-Bag and his wife and the jackaroos. His own hired stockmen and station workers now ate in the kitchen dining room, away from the boss. Sandy recalled Red Hills, where Mary had been the cook and they all sat at the same table talking and joking. It was after the shift to Seven Mile that they had started to eat apart from the hired help. The wheel of fortune really had turned full-circle; himself no more the dusty drover trying to win the heart of the young housemaid fresh from the city.

The stock and station agent was trying to interest him in the purchase of another big station up for sale. The agent, droned on about hard times in the pastoral industry and how this station was a bargain. In spite of himself, Sandy began to think, did he have enough – was he contented, did he want more? He had achieved what he had set out to do years ago and now someone was trying to sell him more. He turned his attention to the roast beef on the table and began to carve the meat; and as he did so he could not help wondering whose beef it was they were about to enjoy.

17

After being with Sandy and Bindi, Mulga visited his home town. Everything had changed. Gone was the yumba, where he had been reared; the Murris now lived in the comfort of town houses alongside the whites. He soon learned that here it was not whites against blacks that separated his people but black against black. Some would complain that others were getting more handouts for instance, or a better house. Stray dogs still roamed the place, but more disturbing to Mulga were the kids, who, like the dogs, ran wild and unchecked around the streets. Despite all the handout money, no-one seemed to want to do anything about these kids. Some already had criminal records a mile long. Although they were only a minority of the Aboriginal populaton, their problems loomed large. They seemed protected yet doomed from the day of their birth, not because of poverty and lack of opportunity in this case, but because of the lack of parental control. They were also helped along their road to destruction by do-gooders, who made excuses for their crimes, as well as the police and a government reluctant to act in case they were seen as racist.

The townspeople themselves were always sweeping things under the carpet, blaming everything but the real cause – the neglect of the kids by their parents. 'Get them jobs!' they screamed. 'Then kids and teenagers won't drink and commit crimes.' But offered jobs, many would not work. Some, like their parents, had become a lost generation reared on the dole. Mulga was pleased to see that the majority of the kids did seek education and jobs. They were the ones unnoticed by the do-gooders and the rest of the community when they talked of those who roamed the streets.

Mulga felt sorrow for these neglected kids who paid the penalty for their parents' inability or unwillingness to adapt to change. Mulga believed that since the dawning of the Dreamtime his people had adapted to change realising that knowledge could only enrich their culture and lifestyle. How many tribes and cultures were wiped out by not adapting? His thoughts were now interrupted by Uncle Joe who declared street kids and crime were everybody's problem.

'So I tell you fellas story. Hey missus,' Uncle Joe asked the barmaid, 'you got pencil and paper?' He had learnt to draw in a cold concrete cell – his crime, unpaid fines. He drew a huge room, in the centre a big table on which was stacked wads of money and valuables reaching almost to the ceiling. Sitting around were people of all nationalities gleefully rubbing their hands. 'That's *Organised Crime* mate, no Aborigines in that mob. All them fellas drive off in flash cars leaving the table and room clean.'

Then Uncle Joe drew a street scene, broken shop windows scattered around, many bottles; only Aborigines in this scene, all fighting each other. They are driven off in police vans, leaving behind only the bottles in the dirty street. 'That's *Disorganised Crime*. What you fellas think, hey?'

Was this old man trying to say something in pictures about the disunity of the tribes, thought Mulga. For a while we remained disorganised and fought over scraps and filled the jails, others reaped the rich rewards – whether it be from crime, mineral rights, grazing rights or land rights. Yet it was not to say Murris should become involved in crime of any sort – simply that they must adapt to the ways of the modern world.

Mulga thought of the generations before him, many had adapted. Unlike the protective missions, in the yumbas of rural towns there were no tea and sugar handouts: it was here the real struggle for improvement and equal wages and rights had been won – not given – years ago. And it had come about through education and the search for knowledge, not through ignorance and hatred.

Now, it seemed to Mulga, everyone wanted to be Aboriginal. He had seen people asking for pieces of paper to verify their Aboriginality, which he thought ironic. Not long ago, in New South Wales and the Northern Territory, Aborigines had to seek pieces of paper to become 'honorary white men' as Mulga and his mates described them. They had never sought papers to show what they were. They knew who they were. Mulga was saddened by the things he saw: little white bureaucrats replaced by black bureaucrats, sitting around a table determining who was Aboriginal and who wasn't, then handing out pieces of paper. To Mulga this was the ultimate insult; one Murri being told by another he was not Aboriginal because he didn't seek handouts, sit in the gutter and drink and spend his time playing cards with the other Murris.

Mulga himself would never seek a piece of paper as proof he was Aboriginal. He could trace his Aboriginal ancestry to the beginning of time and his white ancestry back to Ireland and England. Being Aboriginal was not a piece of paper, as some thought, it was in the mind. His people could become doctors, lawyers, anything. They might never attend a corroboree yet they would be just as much Murri as those who still held to all the tribal beliefs. Some parts of Aboriginal culture and belief were questioned by many thinking people as a bit hard to swallow. Mulga had always stressed if he could find a political party, culture or religious order based on commonsense he would embrace them all. Commonsense, bought about by education, was the key. Then time and the future would determine Aboriginal destiny, not outdated religions or cultural beliefs, black or white. The past could only help if people learned from their mistakes.

Mulga saw his people as though they were divided

into the young, living for the present, and the old, wishing for the past and their lost youthfulness. Now it was time for the so-called wise Aboriginal elders, for the sake of the next generations, to pull their heads out of the sand and face up to reality.

Both Mulga and Bindi and many like them had read some words written on this matter:

one law for all tribes
black, white, and brown
in a land we call heaven:
let's look to the future
while recording the past
with a sharing of culture
in a vision of hope –
for knowledge, not ignorance
will show us the way.

Where the fringe-dwellers used to live, Mulga stood and looked at the scene before him. Where humpies and tents once stood now there were only tall gum trees, huge spreading willows and the old man saltbush that had once hedged the yumba shacks. The coolabah trees that had looked ancient when he was a boy still stood like guardians of the past. Beneath them they had sought shade in the heat of summer. He closed his eyes and the memories came back.

He recalled how the kids and adults played rounders together where the undergrowth and black wattle now grew. Barefoot, the kids raced over the cracked black ground through the bindi-eyes and around the bases, dodging the tennis ball. He pictured the cleared space where the claypan dances were held at Christmas time, when most of the Murris came to town from the stations where they worked. Then for a few nights the yumba came alive as the women swept the ground with their hop bush brooms, sprinkling it with water to make it hard and settle the dust. As the night took over, they would gather, young and old. Musicians with accordions, guitars, bones, spoons and music sticks would begin playing as the lights came on. Mulga remembered those lights well: a couple of kids were sent farther down among the sandhills to the rubbish dump, where they would find worn-out car and truck tyres and roll them back to the yumba. As the music started they would be set ablaze. For hours the tyres burnt into the night and romantic couples danced until the red glow of dawn lightened the sky. Then, as the sun rose, smoke would rise from a dozen camp fires, while around the dance ground, now a dusty claypan once more, great piles of white ash covered big coils of wire – all that remained of the tyres. Like the flames of some romances, they died with the dawn.

Looking over to where the humpies had stood, the trees marking their place, Mulga remembered the evenings, when the yumba became a beehive as people searched for wood or fetched water from the taps hundreds of yards away. Some used old kerosene tins as buckets, others bore long poles like the Chinese across their shoulders with a bucket of water dangling on each end. Showers for the kids were under the tap itself. Even in winter the water from the artesian bore was warm, and at sundown the kids would shower, then race home before they felt the winter cold. At sundown the yumba was alive with mothers calling home their kids, for sundown was a sort of deadline for kids to be home. If they weren't, they usually got a hiding. As the sun got lower and some kids were still missing the mothers' voices became louder. Gradually the last kids straggled home from the sandhills, some dragging dead hop bush for kindling, others from the river where they had been fishing or gathering firewood.

In summer time, they gathered the cow and horse dung for the mosquito fires that would smoulder throughout the night. As he thought of those smoke fires, Mulga wondered which was worse, the modern aerosol or the smoke. Both stopped the mozzie, but at what cost to health. Sitting there in reverie, Mulga fancied he heard the voices of the past, the long loud *coo-ee* of some frantic mother still calling for her kids, then telling them in English and in her own tongue about the dangers that awaited them at night. For many of them, the night still belonged to the dibble-dibble. Then as the night took over he saw again the flickering lights of kerosene and carbide lamps, while others strained their eyes to see amid the shadows cast by the fat lamps. They were the cheapest: all that was needed was a treacle tin, some animal fat, and a piece of felt from some worn-out hat. This was how the lights came on in the yumbas of the

West. After supper, Mulga recalled that sometimes an uncle or aunt would tell of the past, the stories of animals and birds, which ones not to kill, the bad ones and good ones, why one would always be alone, others in pairs and mobs, how they got their colour, why they acted as they did – and the danger of the river when the Munta-gutta was angry …

The Munta-gutta lived in the river, in the deepest part of the big waterhole. The old people would tell where he lived and Mulga had seen the place. He remembered the big droughts, when from beyond the river the thick red dust and sandstorms would come out of the west. Then everything was of murky gloom as the sand and dust storm raged. In the drought the waterholes shrank but never dried up; the water became brown and muddy and beneath the overhanging branches of ti-trees on the farthest bank you could see a rocky outcrop where most Murris refused to fish – for it was in this rocky cavern that the Munta-gutta lived. It was his escape route to other waterholes if this one did dry up. For all the inland lakes and waterholes were connected by these tunnels, according to legend. Mulga recalled that when he and the other kids were warned about the river and the Munta-gutta, they'd always say: 'He won't catch us, we run away on land, Munta-gutta can't follow, he got no feet.' To which the elder would reply: 'He get ya all right, Munta-gutta smarter than you fella kids. If he want to catch you he just call up whirlywind – it come fast, pick you fella up, dump ya in the water. Or he blow on the water, make big waterspout like whirlywind, it come out of river, spinning real fast. It catch you – where you be then, hey?' – 'I get my father's gun, shoot him,' someone would say. – 'Guns no good, boy, bullets can't hurt Munta-gutta.'

Most boys would head for the river away from where the cave was. Mulga remembered old people coming home from fishing in a hurry, claiming they had seen a strange thing in the river, like a huge log floating upstream against the strong wind, without a ripple. And as they fished near the cave there was a large splash, bigger than the splash of any jumping fish. This, they said, was a warning from Munta-gutta that the fish near here were his. So the people would hastily roll up their lines and head for home, some not even bothering to stop to roll their lines up, for they knew the river belonged to the Munta-gutta.

Mulga had listened at night to people telling of seeing the Munta-gutta. He and the other kids listened entranced. Always the description of the Munta-gutta was the same: it was like some miniature Loch Ness monster, they said. People told of sitting on the riverbank and even though the water was not flowing, they saw black muddy water and leaves coming to the surface in a whirlpool: that was the Munta-gutta, they said, cleaning out his home and tunnel that linked all the waterholes of the inland by underground rivers, so when one waterhole dried up Munta-gutta would never perish: he could reappear in another river system miles away. Unless all the waters of the inland dried up he would never die.

What was fact, what was myth Mulga had wondered, an Aboriginal boy going to white school and learning white stories of flying horses, dragons breathing fire, vampires, witches, magicians, angels, people turned to stone ... he'd learned of these things by day and at night he'd learned of the Munta-gutta, dibble-dibbles, the qurra-mutcha and kidicha. In his school books he learned how the stars were named, and at night he learned other stories more credible than the information in the school books: he learned from the Dreamtime legends how the stars came to be. If it was hard for white kids to learn at school, it was doubly hard for the Murri kids. The whites had only to learn their own beliefs and stories, while the Murri had to learn twice as much. At night time around the camp fire he learned other stories of creation more enchanting than a magic carpet ride, how sinners were turned into birds or animals as punishment, while others forever fleeing across the sky became the stars.

For kids like Mulga and Bindi school was not their only classroom. They learned, for instance, to track the animals they still hunted sometimes for food. For them, reading a track was as important as the reading of books. Australia's history was not all written in books, it was written on the ground, recorded long before white settlement by some black historians in cave paintings and carved deep in hard rock in a language that now seemed lost.

And now, as Mulga sat beneath the cedar tree where his home had been, he recalled for one fleeting moment as a boy how he had reached down into the brown muddy water of the river and stroked the Munta-gutta.

He often used to wander off to the river, fishing or wading in the shallow waters. This day, as he played in the water alone, he began to dog-paddle out farther. Moving around, he felt a log about a foot below the muddy surface of the water. He rested for a while on the log, hanging on to it with both hands. Then, realising he should be able to stand up in the shallow water, he reached down to try to feel the river bottom. Instead, his hand felt something alive and damp. For a second he crouched there frozen, then slowly he traced the thing with his fingertips. He realised it was longer than himself ... and to make matters worse there were two of these things lying side by side beneath the log. It must be the Munta-gutta! Mulga gave one mighty leap backwards, turned in mid-air and was running before he landed in about a foot of water. In a few bounds he gained the bank and still running flat-out reached down and gathered up his shirt and trousers, heading for the safety of a big gum tree about fifty yards away. Puffing, he waited until he had caught his breath, then peered out from behind the gum tree. All he could see was the stillness of the brown muddy water and the deep track where he had raced across the sand.

Puzzled, he stood there staring as the water, trying to fathom what he had felt. It *must* have been the Munta-gutta, it was so large. But was it large enough? Maybe there were baby Munta-guttas that came up here to play in the shallow end of the waterhole. It was something Mulga never forgot. He dared not tell anyone about it, for if he told how he had discovered where the Munta-gutta slept he would have been punished for going swimming alone. So for a few years he carried this secret with him.

But when he grew older and had learnt to swim properly, he was taken with the elders one day to drag the river for the big cod fish. The old men would walk along the bank silently, the net carried on poles on their shoulders. Then they would stop and Mulga would hear them speaking to each other about a dead log or certain other places they knew of where the cod slept. Silently they would glide into the water, the net still on their shoulders. When they reached the spot where the cod slept, they would place the net between the cod and the deepest water, drive the poles into the mud and stand at each end of the poles. Then others would circle around, making as much noise as possible and splashing so that the cod would leave his nest and swim into the net, whereupon the men would lift the poles and twisting frantically, one clockwise the other anti-clockwise, the fish would be entangled. Dog-paddling in deep water with the pole resting on their shoulders again, the men would then head for the bank. It was while hunting up the cod fish that Mulga thought he had solved the mystery of the Munta-gutta he had felt years before. While the men waited with the net, Mulga and the others dived and splashed around some dead logs and he was told to feel around the bottom of the log, for sometimes the big old cods wouldn't budge from the nest they had scooped out around the log. As Mulga dived and felt around the log, he repeated that sensation of feeling something damp and alive. He surfaced quickly. 'There's something down there!' he said, his courage boosted by the others splashing around.

He dived once more, and soon his fingertips felt the thing again. He ran his fingertips up and down the soft smooth belly of the cod as it lay still, then surfaced and told the others. Soon they were all diving and the cod, forced out of his bed, raced for the deep water. As he hit the net there were shouts from the men twisting the poles. They carried the net from the water and unravelled it on the bank. Out fell a thirty-pound cod. Mulga stood looking at the cod and stroking its smooth, damp belly for a long while. At last, he thought to himself, the secret of where the Munta-gutta slept was a secret no more: he was sure now that what he had reached down and felt years before was just a couple of big cod fish.

Smiling to himself with this new-found revelation, he rejoiced with the others on the riverbank. They began to argue about whether they should get more fish, but the older ones said they had enough. While they spoke, from the farthest bank came one loud splash, as though a whale had hit the water, and a great wave flowed out from that direction. 'Must be a bloody big limb fallen in the water,' someone said. 'No limb that,' said another, 'no tree along there.' And already the old men were headed up the bank, calling to the others: 'Come on, that *him* telling us to go, not be greedy and take all the fish from river.'

Mulga was as puzzled as ever. He thought he'd solved the riddle of the Munta-gutta, but now that big splash and the old men saying they must go left him confused. He questioned the old men as they rested on the riverbank, and was told the Munta-gutta let the Murris take fish, but if they became greedy he punished them. Suddenly from the far bank came a deep throbbing beat. 'Must be emu over there,' said Mulga – 'Don't be silly, boy,' said one old man, 'emu don't live in river.' Then there was another splash from the river and the others hurried away, heading for home. The drumming sound came again across the water, then another splash ... Mulga turned and raced after the men, his mind in turmoil.

As he recalled the past and sat and stared at the deserted yumba site he felt no great loss in the passing of the lifestyle they lived. His only regret for the passing of that era was that the old people, his parents and others from the yumba were not alive today to share the comforts of modern living. They surely deserved them more than most of those who now wandered around the streets living on handouts yet still wanting more. It seemed to Mulga that 'Gim-me' was now the password of a whole generation reared on the dole, with no reliance on self to achieve anything. This did not apply to all; but as Mulga saw in his travels, some who got out and helped themselves and made the grade in the present were being criticised by those screaming loudest for land rights and more. It seemed that if you did not wave a flag and scream you were on the other side. The fact was that all the problems could be cured by the Aborigines themselves. If all the money spent on meetings was diverted to housing, education and health, what would be the outcome, Mulga often wondered. What was the sense in only Murris meeting and talking among themselves all the time? By doing this, only they would know what they wanted. But by sitting at the table with the rest of the people, kicking them in the shins if necessary, they would get their message across to all.

For every Aborigine that had failed to come to terms with reality there were a hundred who had succeeded; the tragedy was that nowadays these, who could think and reason for themselves, were described as 'coconuts', brown outside and white inside. Mulga thought this was a compliment, not an insult as it was intended to be by some radicals who spoke only for a small minority. Mulga thought it was better to be a 'coconut' than a 'pee-wee's nest', as he named these so-called leaders. A pee-wee's nest was brown all over: mud outside and shit inside.

The people who disagreed with the radicals were not asked to meetings because they might question the decisions made by a few. In this way the poor illiterate Murri on the bottom was being denied a modern education, which would enable him to determine his own destiny. It was the Murri who now discriminated against the Murri, with everything up for grabs. The greediest hands reached highest, and still only crumbs fell to those at the bottom.

Sitting in a pub, Mulga talked and drank with his kinsfolk as they talked of the past, many wishing for the so-called 'good old days'. But none would like to give up the electric light for the fat lamps, or go back to dragging wood and carrying water; none would exchange the comforts of the present, the dole money when unemployed. Walkabout was now a new Toyota, tucker came from a supermarket. The past held fond memories but none would wish to relive them. To the old people who had lived in that era the present was great and some could see a still greater future. The only thing most missed from the past, if they were honest, was their youth. But that was gone forever. So why condemn the present while dwelling on the past? The past was history and would be recorded. It could never be shaped like the future, one old Murri told them as they argued about the 'good old days'. 'Speaking truthfully,' he said, 'I could never claim they were good old days. I have many fond memories of the past, but as for the living and working conditions, I'm glad they are gone forever. I remember one time,' he said with a smile, 'when the boss would put water in the raspberry jam to make it last longer, and we weren't allowed to put butter as well as jam on the one slice of bread.'

Sitting in the pub, some of the Murris argued about what they owed out of social security or pension cheques and who they would shout for. Some sat around waiting for the 'Captain' to cash his dole cheque. A Murri called 'Teaspoon' was Captain today; he had just cashed a big cheque. Mulga remembered the old days when some Murris would sit waiting for the dust-covered stockmen from the stations to arrive with their big cheques and bigger thirsts after months in the bush. Now so many of them waited on a letter and the mailman to bring them cheques. Then for one day they would be Captain, calling the shots. Today a woman walked up to Teaspoon, drunk and loud-mouthed. 'You gonna shout me, ya bastard?' she asked. – 'No,' said Teaspoon, 'ya got ya pay yesterday, ya didn't shout us.'

While the drunken woman argued, another Murri was being barred from the pub. 'Ya bastard, ya always pinching my ashtrays and beer glasses,' the publican said. – 'I'm sorry, mate,' said the Murri. 'I really needed the glasses at home. We only got Vegemite jars to drink our plonk.'

Out at the back of the pub some Murris, mostly women, gathered around a table while their kids hung around, and tried to take each other's money playing cutt-em. Some would walk home with pension or dole cheque lost on the turn of a card, and their electricity and rent bills unpaid. On pension or dole day someone would always win up big, but Mulga observed there was no sharing here of wealth and money: they would take each other for the last dollar.

Yet Mulga was always amazed how the down-and-out Murris could always laugh and joke about their plight. Things the white community regarded as disasters happened every day to the Murri. Laughter was their shield, a protection against despair.

It wasn't the gamblers or the drunken men and women who worried Mulga so much. It was their kids. They were the ones who would inherit the legacy of hopelessness their parents left behind. Their playground was the streets of the town, where they wandered unchecked ... unlike the old days, when a big red sandhill stood like a barrier between those from the town and those from the yumba. Now that barrier had been crossed; black and white lived side by side.

Drinking with his kinsfolk, Mulga put forward the same arguments he used in talking to white people. They had got on to discussing the law. When would people understand that a black criminal was the same as a white criminal, and both should be punished accordingly? he asked. Again, just because someone was a relative, why should he be protected? Crime demanded punishment. But he thought the Murris should be questioning the decisions of white judges and magistrates in relation to crime figures and the sentences handed out to blacks and whites for similar crimes. They should be keeping records, and the law administrators should be answerable to the public for their decisions.

'We have to get smart or get trampled further into the dust,' Mulga told his kinsfolk. He pointed out that there were a lot more African elephants on earth than Murris. Yet the African elephant was listed as an endangered species.

'Maybe the elephants are smarter than us Murris,' Teaspoon remarked, raising a gust of laughter. 'Maybe that's why there's more of them.'

Later on the pub filled to overflowing. Murris had come from far and wide to attend a funeral. Now, the funeral over, they laughed and joked and found solace in the bottle. Later they would start a big card game and some would fight. Nowadays, Mulga thought, Murris seemed to rejoice at death the way the Irish celebrated with a wake. Aboriginal culture in relation to death had certainly changed since he was a boy. He remembered the days in the yumba after a funeral. There was no rejoicing then, only respect for the dead. When his grandmother was alive, after a death in the family he and the other kids were smoked, together with the humpies they lived in, to keep away the restless spirits. Now it seemed that his kinsfolk called on spirits from a bottle to appease the dead. It appeared that for some, a funeral had become a social occasion.

Everything changes – Mulga was well aware of that. He had roamed the land and seen strange things: petrified trees, opalised trees, the long dead fossils of creatures scattered across the plains that were once the bed of an inland sea. He had seen it rain fish in the driest parts of the inland, and sat for hours trying to fathom the tracks embedded deep in rock that was once lava or mud, tracks left behind by now extinct animals and fish, maybe a million years ago. Mulga suspected that thousands of species of animals, fish and birds had disappeared from the face of the earth. How many tribes of people had also disappeared, even here in Australia – how many different groups of humans, falling to adapt, had been replaced by another group? (As a boy, Mulga had seen the last of one such tribe himself. There was an old man who lived alone in the yumba, different in features and colour from any Murri he had seen. He was said by the elders to roam his grandmother's tribal lands.) It seemed that for every species that disappeared, another evolved in its place, more adapted to the changing times.

At night in the bush, Mulga would lie in his swag gazing at the stars and planets and the man-made satellite circling above and think of the endless universe – apart from time, space seemed the only other thing that was endless. He thought of Halley's Comet rushing through space: imagine Mulga catching a ride on Halley's Comet, travelling at thousands of miles an hour, not stopping for a rest, to refuel or change drivers, taking seventy years or so to make its rounds. What a bus ride, Mulga would think from the comfort of his earthbound swag, looking up into the endless void that was space. Sandy's cattle empire, Bindi's tribal empire, even Australia, the world itself, paled into insignificance against the endless universe.

That day, for the thousandth time, Mulga told his Murri mates: 'I'm going to sit down and write a bloody story about all the things I've seen and heard.' – 'Bullshit,' said Teaspoon. 'For years now ya been gonna write a book. Maybe, like me, ya only read brands and earmarks. We'll believe you when we see it, mate.'

18

It was more than forty years since Sandy, Bindi and Mulga had sat around the camp fire on Red Hills Station and planned their muster of the unbranded cattle that roamed the vast, unfenced acres of Mulga Downs. Today, no more the fit young stockman but round and portly, with greying hair, Sandy stood in the garden at Mulga Downs homestead, watching as Mary picked a few flowers for the dining table, while their grandchildren tumbled and rolled over the well tended lawn. He turned to gaze towards the hazy, bluish hills in the distance ... Red Hills, where Bindi was guardian of his tribal land. He remembered how he and Mulga had often found Bindi at the rock hole on Red Hills, sitting silently. They would turn away and leave him there, as Mulga tried to explain that to Bindi the rock hole cave painting and the etchings on the rock were like a shrine: this was his spiritual home.

When Sandy had planned the cattle duffing all those years ago, he had picked Bindi and Mulga, not only because of their blood ties and because they were good stockmen, but because he knew they never spoke of the things they had done, the way most men in town seemed to boast after a drink or two.

On the road outside the garden a couple of stockmen roared past on motorbikes and Sandy frowned. The day of the traditional stockman seemed to be vanishing fast. He had just driven around his vast cattle empire, ruled long ago by old Sugar-Bag. In the back paddock, along the Red Hills boundary, he'd noticed the mobs of unbranded cattle his men had missed in a hurried muster, and once again he was wondering whether he should spend money and fence the big paddock. It would make it easier for his men to muster and brand those cleanskins. Besides, Sandy still wondered from time to time whether Bindi's mob would take a chance, as he himself had years ago, and build up their herd from the unbranded cattle on Mulga Downs. He thought it was best he had retired and didn't know what happened to the cleanskins. All the same, in the morning he would talk to his son and tell him to take more care when mustering the back paddock.

Lately, young Sandy had been talking about other places for sale that would expand the Mulga Downs territory and increase their assets. His son was one of the new breed of stockmen: he also wanted helicopters for mustering. Sometimes, as he read the notices of stations for sale in the rural papers, Sandy was tempted by the notion of expansion. Maybe his grandson would want a station in the future ... Was he really satisfied with what he had achieved in his lifetime, he asked himself. He thought of Mulga, now living in the city again, still owning nothing, still asking questions, still searching for answers, coming and going as he pleased. Once again Sandy wondered who had achieved the most: himself with his cattle empire and his wealth; Bindi as guardian of his tribal land; or Mulga with his independence and his search for knowledge. Sandy smiled as he wondered whether Mulga had started to type the stories he'd always said he would write on that battered old typewriter from the Seven Mile office. What on earth would he write about? Nothing seemed to happen out in the bush ... maybe, he thought, Mulga had wasted his life searching for answers.

Thirty miles away Bindi looked south across the vast expanse of grey-green mulga forest. Without the use of map or road he knew exactly where it lay, hidden from his view by the mulga trees and by shimmering heatwaves that rose from the red-brown land to create that purplish haze that extended just above the tree tops. Bindi could have found his way through the paddocks of Mulga Downs blindfolded. Sometimes, at night, he went back in imagination to every place he had camped when he'd been employed by old Sugar-Bag to muster his cattle legally. He could also visualise the camps which he, Sandy and Mulga had used for their illegal musters of the Mulga Downs unbranded cattle.

Sometimes his son still talked about the big mobs of cleanskins that roamed the back paddock of Mulga Downs — just waiting, he would say, for someone to come along and put a brand on them. Bindi smiled and wondered what Mulga would think about the idea of pinching Sandy's cattle. He'd probably laugh and say that if Sandy couldn't muster his own cattle, then they were up for grabs to whoever could put a brand on them.

Bindi had decided a little while ago that he would take a holiday for a few months, maybe visit the city and his old mate Mulga, leaving his son in charge of Red Hills for a few months. If, during this time, he did happen to help himself to Sandy's unbranded herd — well, that was his business. Somehow he had to make Red Hills pay its way; the station should be stocked as quickly as possible. With no surplus money in hand, maybe it would be best to let the youngsters stock the place as they saw fit. At Red Hills his people came and went on their tribal land; they could come here and keep alive their culture. But Bindi knew that was not enough. It was the lifestyle of his people he worried about now, a lifestyle that saw them die half a lifetime earlier than other Australians, mostly of diseases that were curable. Bindi was convinced that education in the present was just as important as education in the past. It was the reluctance of his people to adapt to a changing lifestyle that was killing them. He was aware, too, of government yes-men, who would do anything so long as the boat was not rocked, and keep on giving handouts so long as you agreed with them. They were another force to be reckoned with.

Bindi thought of the changes in his own lifetime: he remembered the days when he was a boy on Blackwater, scaling barefoot up the horses' shoulders, helping with the musters, his pay sometimes a bag of boiled lollies. He recalled the long nights outback when he, Sandy and Mulga had talked long about the past, the present and the future, the need for understanding between all races, and for the ability to adapt to the changing world. They had argued about everything during those nights, from religion to the price of beer.

Bindi's needs were simple. He had achieved his goal: as custodian of his tribal land a great weight had been lifted from his mind. He had passed on the beliefs and legends handed down from the Dreamtime and his successors would maintain their affinity with the land.

A thousand miles away in the city, Mulga sat in his dingy little flat, staring at his old typewriter. He thought of the many times in the past when he had told his mates, after witnessing some funny or tragic episode in his nomadic life, that he would write about it. How often, he thought, he'd said those words – 'One day I'll write a book about all this'.

Yet now his mind was blank. The floor was littered with discarded sheets of paper. What could he write about?

He thought of the crowded city streets with their teeming masses. He thought of the squalor of the city slums and the loud-voiced tenants who argued and fought in a dozen different tongues. It was a world away from the bawling herds of the branding yards, but it was possible to look on people as a funny brand of cattle or sheep. Yet every one was different. Some stood out: those with t-shirts pushing a cause were like branded cattle, they belonged to someone.

He thought of the quiet, cool art galleries he had visited, the sports fields with their one-eyed screaming fans, the racetracks, watched the gleaming horses, the jockeys in glittering silks, the women decked out in the latest fashions, parading like the horses. As the bookie called the odds, among the crowd the racecourse urger, hat tilted to one side, speaking from the corner of his mouth as he handed out tips: 'Can't be beaten – tell no-one but you – the owner's a friend of mine.' Yet Mulga could not force himself to write of any of these things. He felt restless; so many things came into his mind, but he could not settle down to his typewriter. His thoughts roved across the world. He pondered on the uneasy peace between the Arabs and the Jews, Germany with its reunification, unrest in Russia, the strife of political and religious groups everywhere. He thought of the past, of how much his own life had changed over the years, from the yumba with its smoky fat lamps and cow dung fires to his present surroundings of electric lights, TV and running water. Things regarded as essential items today had been luxuries in the old days. His world had changed, and for the better. Yet he recalled the past with fond memories, despite the struggle it contained.

Inevitably, his thoughts turned to his own people, and once again he wondered just where some so-called Murri leaders were taking them. Back to the past was his guess — how many times had he argued that education should come before land rights, otherwise in a hundred years' time, even if every Aborigine was given a thousand acres, it would not solve his health or housing problems. As Bindi had said, once there were ancient Aborigines; now there are modern Aborigines. Mulga had never been to the USA or Canada, where the Indians had been granted land rights for over two hundred years. But he could make a guess as to who were the most disadvantaged people in both countries, in terms of health, housing, education and work.

He knew that some people accused him of sitting on the fence where Aboriginal issues were concerned. But Mulga knew all about barbed wire fences: if you tried to step through them your shirt got torn, if you tried to step over them the fork was torn out of your pants. He had learned long ago to walk along the fence until he found a gap or a gate, and then walk through.

He picked up the newspaper and studied the racing guide. Maybe he could write about the fortunes won and lost ...

At last he rose from his chair and, feeling hungry, decided to cook himself a piece of soft, tenderised, tasteless steak he had paid a fortune for in the supermarket. As he watched the meat cook, he thought what he would give to taste once more the steak or corn beef of Mulga Downs or Red Hills. He turned the meat, wondering whether it could possibly be part of some old piker bullock from out West ...

And then he thought: why not write a book about what he knew best – the outback, the men and women who lived and worked there, the bad times and the good, the laughter and the sorrow. He took a bite from the tasteless steak, decided that it had never seen Mulga Downs or Red Hills, and tossed it in the garbage tin. Then he walked to his typewriter, sat down and began to write the story of three bushmen, once great mates together, who now sat at different tables and wondered whose meat it was they ate ...